D0260278

A MESSAGE FROM CHICKEN HOUSE

You'll love this strange and rather brilliant adventure about tall tales, belonging and finding friendship. There *is* a lot about fish, boats, barnacles and the sea – but there's also a lot about family and finding your feet (well, flippers). Fishy jokes aside, Richard Pickard won my special chairman's prize at our *Times*/Chicken House Children's Fiction Competition because I'd never read such an original, funny and bonkers story – it won first *plaice* with me, you might say . . .

BARRY CUNNINGHAM
Publisher
Chicken House

THE PECULIAR TALE OF THE

TENTACLE
BOY

Richard Pickard

Chicken
House

2 PALMER STREET, FROME
SOMERSET BA11 1DS

Text © Richard Pickard 2021
Cover illustration © Maxine Lee-Mackie 2021

First published in Great Britain in 2021
Chicken House
2 Palmer Street
Frome, Somerset BA11 1DS
United Kingdom
www.chickenhousebooks.com

Chicken House/Scholastic Ireland, 89E Lagan Road, Dublin Industrial Estate,
Glasnevin, Dublin D11 HP5F, Republic of Ireland

Cover and interior design by Steve Wells
Cover illustration by Maxine Lee-Mackie
Typeset by Dorchester Typesetting Group Ltd
Printed and bound in Great Britain by CPI Group (UK) Ltd, Croydon CR0 4YY

FSC
www.fsc.org
MIX
Paper from
responsible sources
FSC® C020471

1 3 5 7 9 10 8 6 4 2

British Library Cataloguing in Publication data available.

PB ISBN 978-1-913322-39-7
eISBN 978-1-913696-10-8

For Lucy and James

CHAPTER ONE

Liar

Marina Minnow loved to tell tales. How else was a girl supposed to have any fun in a quiet seaside town like Merlington? The place was so uneventful that the local paper was dominated by the yo-yoing prices of pollock, and so obsessed by fish that on the seafront alone there were seventeen fishmongers all vying for power. In Marina's opinion, having to grow up somewhere as dull as Merlington without any imagination was a fate worse than death.

Most people knew they had to take what Marina said with a pinch of salt. 'She'll be a great writer one day,' her mother Sally would tell strangers as they walked down the beach, Marina loudly translating the cries of a seagull or musing on the alien origins of a peculiar-looking shell. Though it was a budding talent in her mother's eyes, Marina's tales drove some people round the twist, especially her school friends and their narrow-minded parents. She would never set out to cause harm with her stories, or to intentionally mislead someone – but the trouble was she could be quite convincing.

At the last summer fair, when her classmate Peter Featherfin had polished off a family-sized eel pie all by himself, Marina had launched into such an extraordinary tale that he'd been convinced he would wake the next morning with a jellied stomach and puff pastry hair. 'You'll turn into an eel pie!' she'd cried, as he licked the last crumbs from the plate. Marina had been dragged from her bed and round to the Featherfin home to apologize, so that Peter too might finally get some sleep. It always seemed worthwhile, though, as the thought of life in Merlington without a healthy dose of drama was more boring than Marina could possibly imagine!

It was never exactly busy, but by October the town was dead. Today, just a few solitary fishermen lined the surf as they pulled in their final haul of the day – crabs, plaice and shrimp – and the multicoloured fronts of the shabby beach huts glinted in the fading sun. Marina and her classmates, Edie, Wendy and Daisy, had been wandering aimlessly through the cobbled streets since school had finished an hour earlier, picking at a polystyrene tray of soggy chips. Now they weaved a ragged path along the beach of shells and pebbles, which ran from the pub at the harbour's edge to the cliffs that rose sharply from the water once the shore was lost at high tide.

Marina could feel the story on the tip of her tongue before she even knew what it was.

'Make sure you throw that tray in the bin,' she called to Wendy Whitby, a know-it-all girl with sharp features like a bird. 'If it's washed into the sea, a jelly-fish might fall in love with it. You'll only be helping to break the poor thing's heart in the end.'

'What are you talking about?' asked Wendy,

rolling her eyes. 'It's a piece of rubbish, why would a jellyfish think it was another jellyfish?'

'They don't have eyes; how could they know? Jellyfish are sensitive creatures,' Marina insisted.

Edie laughed, sensing the elaborate story which was building in her best friend's mind.

'I heard that fish sometimes get stuck in those plastic six-pack rings for beer cans,' said Daisy Baitman, a quiet girl who rarely got involved in Marina and Wendy's disagreements. As soon as she realized that she'd spoken up, her mouth dropped into a perfectly formed 'o' and she hid her face behind her braids, backing silently away from the group.

'That's true!' insisted Marina. 'Humans are always invading the ocean and causing damage to the delicate life. There was once an eel ...'

Oh, here we go, thought Wendy.

'... a huge, great, slimy rope of an eel that sat still for almost a decade. He'd hang his head from the nook of his cave and hardly move for anything. Tiny fish would swim by and not even know he was there before they suddenly found themselves halfway down his throat. The eel sat still for so long he was almost welded to the rock, making a wonderfully comfy home for barnacles. Weeks, months, years would pass, and he'd barely open his eyes – just his mouth, which opened and closed with the tide. It wasn't until one day, when a deep-sea diver was exploring the reef, that the eel, in a moment of curiosity, opened his eyes to be greeted by the man's huge glass diving helmet. But the eel didn't even notice the man. All he could see in the dark polished mask was his own quizzical face reflected straight back. He'd never seen another eel before, having not left his cosy cave in such a long time. He didn't even know what it was he was seeing, but he immediately fell in love.

'Yet it was in that moment that the diver turned, flapping his strange plastic feet, and made a break for the surface. Up, up, up, he swam in a cloud of bubbles. The eel did not know *what* to think, or know where his new love had gone, but for the first time in what felt like for ever he swam. He swam free of his rocky home, tearing a whole miniature village apart around him as barnacles and seaweed flew aimlessly through the water. He swam after the diver as fast as he could, as the world ahead grew brighter and warmer than he'd ever thought possible. His cloudy, tired eyes ached at the light, but he knew nothing except the fear he'd never get to see that beautiful face again. Then, as the strange rippling surface came into view the light was blotted out by a huge shape on the water and . . .

'Nothing.

'The eel thrashed and pulled but he was no longer in control of his own movements. He was being dragged out of the sea in a rough, heavy net, and hoisted into the cold air that whipped his skin painfully.'

Marina's friends stood around her in a tight semicircle, their mouths hanging open as she hooked them to attention. All except for Wendy, who had wandered slightly down the beach and had taken to throwing chips at a dozing seagull in irritation.

'What happened to him?' cried Thea Marigold, a small girl from the year below who had joined the group mid-story with an unseasonably huge strawberry ice cream.

'He was thrown in a cool box and driven down the Thames,' continued Marina, matter-of-factly. 'He ended up at the Dagenmoor pub in east London. Three pounds for a pie and mash on Mondays.'

At this final indignity, Wendy, who was daughter

of the local pub landlord, could take it no longer. 'That is a complete load of rubbish!' she cried. 'How could you possibly know all of that? You've never even been to London.'

'She's right,' Daisy added, having found her confidence again. 'My parents take me there every Christmas and a pie and mash would cost way more than that.'

'It so is true,' snapped Marina. 'Everything in London is half-price on Mondays – it's because the city workers all take a packed lunch of their leftover Sunday roast.'

'I can't bear it any more!' bellowed Wendy, scowling at the group. 'Eels, beer cans, polystyrene tubs . . . I'm sick of all your stupid stories. Why can't you live in the real world like the rest of us? Your mum is just another fishmonger, like everyone else in this town. Why do you think you're so special?'

Marina could feel the back of her neck beginning to grow hot.

'Wendy, give it a rest,' Edie begged, running a hand through her long, dark hair in frustration. 'You know it's just a bit of silly fun.'

'It isn't fun, though,' Wendy barked, turning to

Marina. 'All you do is tell great big lies, and everyone laps it up.'

'I think they're funny,' smiled Thea.

'That's because you're a child!' cried Wendy, knocking Thea backwards – a dollop of ice cream dropped to the floor with a sloppy squelch. 'The whole town lets her get away with murder. She thinks she can make up any old story and everyone will just believe it. And you guys think she's funny? Well, I think she's a no-good liar. A *liar*!'

'I am *not* a liar!' burst out Marina, anger surging through her bones. Without even realizing, she had picked up a clump of wet seaweed from the ground and it was flying through the air before she could do a thing about it. A shrill scream rang across the water as the seaweed hit Wendy square in the face with a damp splosh.

CHAPTER TWO

A Light on the Waves

'I cannot believe you *did* that!' gasped Wendy, scrubbing the slime from her cream-coloured dress. 'You are going to pay for this to be cleaned, you freak. You've totally ruined it! What is wrong with you?'

Marina's throat began to grow tight, as her cheeks turned a warm, red hue. She hadn't exactly *meant* to throw the seaweed, but it had already left her hand before she'd noticed. Being called a liar really, really hurt. *Maybe because you think it's true*, a voice in her head suggested quietly. She squashed down the thought.

'It's only a dress,' she said tightly.

'I'm sure it'll come out in the wash,' Edie backed up her friend. 'You don't need to bother with the dry-cleaners.'

'I'm usually *covered* in seaweed after I've been picking periwinkles on the breakwater,' offered Thea, as she wiped pink ice cream from her shoe with a tissue. 'My mum rubs fish grease into the stains and it comes out fine!'

This only managed to further enrage Wendy. 'Now you want me to rub *grease* into my dress?' she screeched, staring down at the green tinge which had settled on her lacy collar.

Marina couldn't help herself.

'Vinegar works well too,' she said, her brain fighting her mouth for control of the words that were spilling from her lips. 'Mrs Cuttle swears by it! She saves all of the soggy newspaper after eating her fish and chips.'

'We aren't babies any more,' Daisy said, stepping

forward to stand beside Wendy. 'We don't need you to make up all these bedtime stories for us like Thea.'

'Especially when they're such stupid lies,' Wendy jeered.

Thea stood up again, almost half the size of the other girls as she stuffed an ice-cream-stained tissue in her pocket. 'I'm not a baby, I just think Marina's got a good imagination.'

'And where's the harm, Wendy?' Edie asked. 'I don't see why you have to be so harsh.'

'Because it's about time you all grew up,' Wendy continued. 'And then, perhaps Marina will be able to tell a story that's actually true for a change.'

Marina felt as though her heart might burst with rage. Instead of waiting to find that another clump of seaweed had somehow appeared in her hand, she turned and ran. Her anger carried her across the wooden groynes that divided the shore and sank down into the rising tide. She climbed each one before thumping on to the sand behind, as the beach of shells and dried seaweed sloped away from the town. The toots of distant cars and the cries of salt-sodden fishermen slowly faded away, along with the voices of Wendy and her friends.

Climbing from the water in the distance ahead was the half-destroyed old pier, a battered landmark which signalled the end of the town's periphery and the beginning of miles of barren beach. The long walkway which had once connected to land had collapsed into the cold sea years ago, following a ravenous fire. Now, the pier's blackened remains rose steeply from the water at its halfway point. At the end was a mould-ridden shack, which had once been a small fishermen's bait shop. The structure swung steadily in the stirring waves on four precarious legs, and Marina idly noticed the tiny windows casting a faint glare on the water as it swayed. Or was it her imagination once again?

People said the bait shop was haunted. All of the fishermen avoided the place, keeping their boats at a distance and dodging the murky waters nearby. Marina had heard the stories – of peculiar shadows on the sea and the strange, snapping sounds which carried through the darkness . . .

No, enough stories for one night.

Marina stomped through the sand towards the shallows, crushing shells and kicking at stray seagulls as she went. Suddenly, she became aware that she was being followed. Turning around sharply to give

Wendy a good what-for, her eyes were met instead by the smiling face of Edie.

'Did you see how angry Wendy was?' she said, suppressing giggles as she bit her bottom lip. Marina's irritation melted at once. Amusement bubbled inside her and before long, the two girls had fallen to the sand in fits of laughter.

'That was incredible!' cried Edie. 'She'll be fuming for days over that stupid dress! She thinks she's so grown up and important.'

'I don't know why I did that,' snorted Marina, righting herself on the damp ground as she winced at the memory of their argument. Being called a liar still hurt.

Edie appeared to sense what was on her friend's mind. 'Don't listen to that misery guts. I really like your stories.'

'You do?'

'Definitely. I wish I could come out with some of the stuff you dream up.'

'You don't think I'm a liar, then?'

'Well . . . I don't think you're a liar. But you're not telling the truth either, are you? I mean, obviously they're just stories . . .'

Marina started to wonder whether Wendy might have a point. Was a true story really worth more than one from her imagination? Nothing that happened in Merlington was nearly as interesting as what she could make up herself. Her dad had always loved sharing stories . . . But that was years ago. Was it something that she had to grow out of?

As she considered this, Edie took her hand and began to lead her back in the direction of town, where the streetlights were now humming to life along the boardwalk. She took a deep breath and began to concede defeat, when something in the corner of her eye caught her attention. A glimmer of orange on the dim water.

The shack on the pier, again. She hadn't imagined it this time – the faintest of lights flickering through two lonely windows, their large cracks visible even from the dusty shore.

'Did you see that?' she asked, spinning on the spot and wondering if she might be going mad. And then . . . 'There! There it is again. Did you see it? It was a light.'

'A light?' asked Edie in confusion. 'But there's nothing out there, no ships.'

'It's coming from the end of the old pier,' Marina insisted. She was caught in a trance, staring out at the gloomy building as it rocked hypnotically on its four rickety legs, waiting for the slightest sign that she was right.

'That's impossible, Marina. The pier hasn't been used since before we were born.'

'I *saw* light, coming from the window! Someone is in there!'

'This isn't because of all those ghost stories, is it?' Edie asked, exasperated. 'I know some of the fishermen think the bait shop is haunted. They all steer clear of the place, telling stories about strange noises and stuff. But, Marina, *it's just another story*.'

Marina felt a sharp jolt of pain as though Edie's words had jabbed her in the ribs.

'There was no light,' Edie continued. 'It's too far away to see anything from here, and it must be rotten solid inside. Who'd be in there now? And how would they have even got there?'

Edie was probably right. No one could live out in that salt-beaten wreck of a building, cut off from the world . . . *could they*? Marina knew that it was already too late. Her mind was running wild with possibilities. She had to know either way.

Everyone thinks I should grow up, she thought. *Well, after this, I'll prove that I can tell a true story too.*

Edie stood aghast as Marina tumbled back down the beach, a low crash of thunder echoing in the distance.

'You're not actually going out there, are you? You're insane!' she yelled, as Marina hauled a rusty rowing boat across the beach with the sound of grinding shells.

'I have to know what's inside.'

'But it's not safe!'

'Wendy says my stories are lies, and even you don't think they could be true. Well, I'm going to start making real life just as exciting instead!'

The tide was coming in quickly as she pushed the boat into the shallow surf, her feet lapped by the encroaching waves. Hopping inside, she thanked her lucky stars she'd worn wellies that morning; the floor of the boat was still wet with slime from a seagull's leftover lunch.

In the invading darkness Marina slipped easily from Edie's sight. She was already invisible among the waves, even quicker than her friend had feared as the tiny boat was swallowed by the swelling sea.

It was then, with a stomach-clenching gasp, that Edie noticed a very quick flicker of light in the corner of her vision. Now the worry of Marina's fate on the rough sea was trampled by a far greater one – about what might, in fact, be waiting for her inside that shack.

CHAPTER THREE

At the Pier

With all her might, Marina pulled the decaying oars of her boat through the waves. Suddenly she felt very stupid. How could she have thought that this would ever end well? Rowing out to sea on a whim, to the abandoned old pier that no one had visited in more than a decade! Her mother would be furious. Marina pushed that thought to the bottom of her wellies and focused on the task at hand. It was too late to worry about any of that now, and there was no point in turning back. At the very least, tomorrow at school she'd be able to boast about visiting the crumbling shack on stilts – she'd bring back a piece of wood as proof, to wave victoriously in Wendy's face. She even had Edie to vouch for her. No one could call her a liar this time.

Finally, Marina reached what remained of the crippled pier's wooden promenade, which rose sharply from the sea like a ladder. She tied a simple knot with the boat's mooring rope and hooked it over a large rusty nail, securing the vessel to the pier as best she could while she bobbed on the water.

Climbing carefully on to the step-like planks, she felt very unsafe on the precarious wood which was sodden and damp beneath her feet. Suddenly, a loud bang sounded from inside the bait shop, echoing across the sea. What little light Marina had glimpsed through the cracked walls disappeared in the same instant. She froze, her heart pounding.

She'd been right – someone was inside!

Now was the moment to prove that she could have a real-life adventure. She clambered up the remaining steps of the decrepit promenade towards the bait shop, and with one swift motion, her breath caught in her chest, she swung the door open on to darkness. The smell of saltwater hit her square in the face, the stench of the sea, of cockles, shells and fish, fresher and stronger than a walk past any one of the town's seventeen fishmongers on a Friday morning. The room lay still – that is, until the rotten door itself collapsed from its hinges with a great thump to the floor, causing Marina to jump. She steadied her nerves, before plucking up the courage to call out.

'Hello?'

No one answered, the sound of her voice absorbed quickly by the damp walls. Who did she actually *think* would have answered? Had she imagined that light all along? Had the moon played a trick on her eyes?

But then, as if from nowhere, came a sound like scratching. A crab, scuttling across the floor and snapping its claws. Or maybe something else . . . A ghost? Was the bait shop really haunted, like the fishermen's stories said? Marina swallowed, her throat dry from the musty, stale air. *Possibly*. Whatever it was, she knew, deep down, that something was with her, hiding in the darkness.

'I know you're there,' she called.

And then, a strange shape formed before her eyes. A boy? A being that held the faintest outline of one, but . . .

Marina dared to inch closer, as the figure stepped into the moonlight. She stared in wonder at the creature's skin, which seemed almost translucent – the skin of a ghost. He crouched down before a small light flickered on. A candle, the one that Marina must've glimpsed from the beach. Her eyes widened as she saw that the boy's skin wasn't skin at all, but a cloak of pearly scales that began at his feet and grew more sparse as they rose up his chest. The scales glittered as the flame danced across them in a blaze of iridescent colour.

It was then that Marina noticed he was holding the candle not with a hand, but in a crab-like pincer – as smooth and hard as stone, and sharp-looking too. His other free pincer clack-clacked in a way that would have been rather menacing had it not been clear he was just as frightened as she was at this very moment. Marina felt her fingers tremble, mimicking his rust-coloured claw. She lifted her eyes to his face.

'Whoa . . .' she breathed.

She saw that his hair was not hair, but a mop of eight slippery tentacles which fell gracefully from a rubbery scalp, swinging at his neck in time with the rocking stilts of the pier. Each tentacle was covered in suckers that pulsated with a curious energy.

Marina swallowed hard again, found her courage, and spoke.

'Don't be afraid,' she said, angry at herself for the crack in her voice. The strange boy started at the sound. 'I'm sorry, I didn't mean to disturb you. I didn't think anyone could possibly be out here.'

The scale-covered creature shifted awkwardly on his feet. He appeared to understand.

'Who are you?' Marina asked. 'What's your name? Do you live out here? How long have you been hiding here all alone?'

Marina realized that she was probably overwhelming the boy with questions, which came from her mouth almost as quickly as they arrived in her head. She took a step backwards and resolved to take it slowly.

'Forget all that, let's start again. What is your name?'

'William,' he said after a pause. His voice was soft,

but broken, like when you speak for the first time on a Saturday morning and surprise yourself with an unused croak. William's voice couldn't have been used for a very long time. He spoke again.

'I've lived here for ages. For as long as I can remember, anyway.'

'You've lived here for ages?' repeated Marina in disbelief. 'How is that possible? How has no one known?'

William shrugged his pasty grey shoulders. 'I'm good at staying out of sight, and none of the sailors ever come near the pier.'

Because they think the place is haunted, thought Marina. 'But how did you get here in the first place?'

'I was brought here when I was a baby.'

'You were brought h—'

Marina was baffled. How could any of this be real? Had something snapped in her brain – had she lost the plot? Or had she fallen asleep and entered one of her own fanciful tales? It all *seemed* real enough. She pinched herself to be sure.

The sharp bite of pain that pulsed down her arm felt very real.

CHAPTER FOUR

William

'I'm sorry, William, this is all so strange that I forgot my manners. My name is Marina.' She extended her hand in greeting, before remembering he only had pincers. In order to avoid a nasty injury, she rather uncoolly pulled back her arm and ran her hand down one of her thick plaits. Luckily, William didn't seem to know what a handshake was in any case.

'It's nice to meet you too, Marina. It's been a very long time since anyone came to see me,' he said with a hint of relief.

Marina's eyes adjusted to the shadows of the candlelight as she surveyed the room – the blackened, mouldy floorboards that seemed to peel like shedding skin; the ceiling which dripped stagnant, murky water with a pitiful *plink plonk*. On one wall hung a crooked painting of some sailing boats, dark grime creeping into the picture from the corners of its frame.

'Imagine if people knew that you'd been out here all alone! They would be in for quite a shock.' Marina smiled warmly, looking at William's friendly face and wondering how she could have ever found him frightening. 'I hope you don't mind me saying, but it's pretty dingy in here.'

'The fisherman tried to lighten it up,' he said, pointing to the soggy painting and a few ancient toys which rotted in the corner. 'I love it. It's home, you know?'

'I guess,' she supposed. 'Is the fisherman the one who brought you here?'

'Yes,' replied William happily. The thought

seemed to cheer him, as he placed the candle back on the windowsill. 'Do you know him?'

'Do I know the fisherman?' Marina asked, perplexed. 'I know lots of fishermen. My whole town is fishermen. Well, there are a fair few fishmongers too – seventeen, in fact, and that's just on the two main streets.'

William's good mood appeared to falter at this news, and he sank down in defeat, plopping on to a mass of old nets which were heaped together into something that resembled a bed. If Marina's arrival had inspired a glimmer of excitement in the strange boy, she had just extinguished it.

'Is there a particular fisherman you're looking for?' she asked, racking her brain for an idea but clutching at straws.

'The only fisherman I've ever known,' he sighed, ripping a stained blanket from a small pile of sheets, each one shredded with claw marks and wet with green moss. 'He's my father.'

His *father*? Marina couldn't imagine that there would be anyone in the entire town who could claim this boy as their son. Merlington was synonymous with fish. It was all they learnt about at school and pretty much the only thing anyone ate, but William was something that even Harold Mole, the greasiest of all the fishmongers in town, couldn't possibly dream up.

'I've been waiting for my father to come back for a really long time. I don't know what could have happened to him.'

Swallowing hard once more, Marina took a step forward. She reached out tentatively, taking a great big claw in her hand. It felt heavy and solid on her palm.

'I understand how you feel, William,' she said. 'My dad has been gone for a long time too.'

Marina's father, Nigel Minnow, had not been seen since a little before his empty fishing net had bobbed up into the surf one stormy evening six winters earlier. Marina's mother and the town as a whole had accepted the inevitable, but Marina was convinced he was still out there. She would frequently dream up lots of brilliant and increasingly eccentric explanations for his survival.

'Where did he go?' asked William curiously. He felt a sudden warmth for the strange girl with her bizarre, lifeless hair and tiny hands.

'Nobody knows,' croaked Marina. 'He was lost at sea during a storm. No one believes he survived, but I know he's out there somewhere. Perhaps a pod of friendly dolphins rescued him from the water, and delivered him safely to a desert island in the English Channel. Now he's just trying to figure out how to get back to the mainland.'

William patted a spot on the pile of nets beside him and motioned for Marina to sit down, which she did, trying not to think about the stain they'd leave on the seat of her trousers.

'I guess we're in the same boat,' smiled William. 'Kippers from the same can!'

'You know, for a boy who's made of fish your English is pretty great,' Marina said with admiration. 'Especially when you consider you've been living on this mouldy pier all on your own! I knew going to school was a waste of time,' she huffed.

'Well, I love to read,' beamed William. He lifted back a few layers of the netting and rummaged through a dirty pile of tin cans hidden beneath. He proffered one to Marina.

She took the can from his extended claw, and read the faded label: 'Lightly smoked sardines, extra virgin olive oil, salt, dried garlic, herbes de Prov . . .' she stuttered. 'Herbes de Pro . . .'

'Herbes de Provence,' interrupted William, who recited from memory in delight as Marina passed back the can. 'This is one of my favourites. I found it in the water a few months ago.'

'You rescued all of these old tins from floating about in the sea? That's awful.'

'Well, it's nice to have some new reading material. Tins are best as everything else just gets soggy and disintegrates. I've had to keep rereading the ones my father brought over so I love finding things, though I did once get one of those plastic six-pack rings for beer cans stuck in my tentacles.'

'Daisy was *right*!' cried Marina, thinking back to the beach and their conversation with Wendy, which felt like a lifetime ago. She pulled herself up from the floor, went to the window and peered towards the seafront which was now shrouded in darkness.

It was late – Mum would be worried if she wasn't home soon – and the storm was starting to get really bad. Suddenly the shack swayed violently on its stilts as thunder crashed overhead, far too close for comfort.

'William, I'm so sorry,' said Marina. 'I have to get back on land before I'm trapped here by the storm. Once I get home, I'll do my best to find out everything I can about your father.'

She climbed through the door and into the cold, wet night, before pausing to look back at William who still sat atop his mountain of nets.

'I promise I'll come and see you again soon.'

'And you'll really look for my father?' he called after her.

'I promise. I promise I'll do everything I can to find him!'

'Oh! Thank you, Marina,' said William, who now stood at the doorway, looking out into the night. 'Thank you for coming to see me on your little boat.'

Marina smiled at him as she waited for the pier to rock closer to her boat. Seizing the moment, with a silent prayer, she leapt through the rain with squinting eyes and landed inside on her back in a heap.

Almost immediately the rope mooring her vessel to the pier snapped free, the half still pinned to the stairs flailing in the wind. Before she could process what was happening, the boat was swept into the darkness – away from the pier, and more terrifyingly, away from the shore.

'No!' she shouted, panic gripping her tightly while she scrambled on her knees, furiously searching for the oars. Her eyes were blinded by the rain, her ears echoing with the howling wind as the boat rolled dangerously on the sea, water smashing against its hull like heavy rocks.

At last, Marina found the familiar shape of her oars in the gloom and heaved them over the edge. She started to row, fighting against the tide, the waves, the elements themselves . . .

The elements won. Suddenly her oars were gone, pulled from her grip by the weight of the water. She screamed with all her might as the roaring winds and the rushing sea swept her further and further from the safety of dry land.

CHAPTER FIVE

Another Tall Tale

'Hold on tight!' a strange voice cried as the waves pitched Marina's boat in the blackness. She felt the vessel shift its course, before it dawned on her that she could once again make out the lights of the shore through the downpour. That the shore seemed to be getting closer!

William was there, at her side in the water, gripping the bow of the boat in his left pincer as he kicked his legs, propelling them towards land. Marina watched as his feet moved through the waves in a flurry, his dazzling scales reflecting the dim moonlight in a kaleidoscope of colour as he battled against the storm with all of his might. In no time at all, before it had seemed humanly possible (but then, was he human?), the boat was grinding to a halt in the shells of the surf with a crunch.

Marina hauled herself out of the treacherous boat and flopped on to the beach with a big sigh of relief. How stupid she had been, to row out to sea without a care in the world. And all to impress Wendy Whitby! Once she had caught her breath, Marina turned to thank her heroic rescuer, only to find that he had already disappeared into the storm. Lucky, it seemed, as suddenly there was Edie, running down the promenade and across the sand screaming her name.

'Marina, where have you been? I've been going out of my mind!' she cried through the rain. Marina could barely hear her as she continued to talk at a million miles an hour. She was in shock, hypnotized by the tentacle boy. Had it really all happened?

'Marina, are you listening?' Edie snapped, breaking

the trance. 'I asked you what you've been doing out there.'

Marina rubbed wet sand from her clothes, which only led to her palms getting covered in annoying, sticky granules. Edie barely paused long enough for her to answer.

'How did you ever manage to row back? A few more minutes and I would have had to call the coast-guard, even if it meant that you were grounded for the rest of time. What happened?'

'You wouldn't believe me if I told you,' she said.

Edie plucked her friend from the ground and pulled her along the promenade under a huge polka-dot ladybird umbrella. Rain hammered the wooden roofs of the beach huts they passed, in a blur of pastel pink, blue and yellow, while the waves continued to crash into the beach with a roar that echoed across the cliffs.

'Come on, you have to tell me,' Edie begged. 'You were out there for absolutely ages. What the hake have you been doing all this time?'

As they reached the stone bridge at the end of the beach, beneath the glowing lights of The Laughing Trout pub, Marina was unable to keep the story to herself any longer. Leaving the seafront and beginning to walk up the abandoned high street, she told her friend everything. Of her incredible encounter with William. Of the decaying pier and the pile of mouldy old toys. Of crab claws and shimmering skin, and the most wonderful head of tentacles.

'Oh, honestly,' spat Edie when the story caught up with the present. 'I've been worried sick and you're giving me a story? I thought you said you'd start making real life an exciting adventure of its own.'

'Wait, what . . . ?' spluttered a confused Marina. They came to a stop on the deserted main road, the last of the many fishmongers now closed and in darkness. Rainwater mingled with the day's tossed-out chips of ice, which were quickly melting in the gutter and beginning to flow down the road like a smelly river. 'I *am* telling the truth. This really happened! You saw me go out there yourself, with your own two eyes. You just dragged me up from the edge of the sea!'

'Yes, and that's all very impressive. But there can't have been anything inside that shack except a couple of crabs and some rotten old buckets of bait – it's just another tall tale. Unless . . .' Edie squinted at Marina in the semi-darkness. 'Are you sure you didn't hit your head on an oar or something? Maybe we should go to the doctor's house and let him check you out.'

She grabbed Marina's face with a free hand, pushing back her eyelids. She held them open with her thumb and forefinger, peering closely at her friend's black pupils which quickly constricted in the streetlight.

'I haven't hit anything.' Marina batted her away. 'I'm telling the truth! Why would I make it up? *How* could I make it up? A kid with crab claws?' She fell back on to a pile of crates that were stacked outside Harold Mole's shop, Mullet Over, which was shielded from the rain by a pinstriped canvas canopy. She'd been sure that Edie would believe her, if no one else. 'I know it sounds insane, but it really happened. His name is William and he's one of the nicest people I've ever met.'

A curtain twitched irritably in the window above, as a bright light briefly illuminated Edie's sceptical face. 'How could a boy have the claws of a crab? It's just not possible.'

'But, Edie, I promise you,' pleaded Marina. 'I'm deadly serious this time, I swear it. I've said that I'll help him find his father but I'm not sure I can do it on my own.'

'So, there's a fully-grown fish man out and about in Merlington too?' Edie laughed, rolling her eyes with an exaggerated flourish. 'What about his mother? Maybe she was that really big haddock Jasper Jenkins caught on Tuesday.'

'I know you think my head's all waterlogged, but they must be out there somewhere! I really need your help. I swore I'd look, and I don't know where to begin!'

Eventually, Marina let it go. She knew how ridiculous it sounded. She could barely believe the encounter herself. Instead, the two girls continued their damp walk home in silence, huddled together under Edie's garish umbrella as the rain cascaded down the sides, encasing them in a cocoon of falling water.

As the shopfronts of fishmongers slowly merged into rows of brightly painted houses with huge windows and balconies of white slatted wood, Marina resolved to prove William's existence at the earliest possible occasion.

Little did she know at that moment, it would take no effort on her part at all.

CHAPTER SIX

Lemon Sole

Marina slept terribly that night – tossing and turning like the turbulent waves that filled her dreams. After a stunted slumber that was rocked by visions of lovelorn eels and tentacle shampoo, she woke with a start at three in the morning and found that everything was normal. Her bedside clock ticked along, waves broke on the shore in the distance, and the soft hum of a solitary speedboat drifted through her bedroom window. It was as though nothing had changed, and yet for Marina, nothing was the same. Not now she knew the fantastical truth – out there in the ocean, the most wondrous of creatures existed.

It was during her restless night that Marina remembered a story. Well, just a glimmer of a story. One that her grandmother had shared when she was younger – a tale of a fisherman and his catch. A bizarre and brilliant catch. The fisherman thought he'd found a measly evening's haul before he'd looked further into his net and realized what lay among the cold, shiny cockles besides an old leather boot . . .

Frustratingly, Marina couldn't remember the details. She was sure that it had something to do with hair like tentacles. It had been one of the last stories Granny Minnow had ever told her, not very long after her father went missing, and before her memory had slipped away. Now Granny barely recognized her, and their visits filled with laughter, tall tales and imagination had become a thing of the past.

But the fisherman's catch had just been another wild story. Nobody except Marina had been out to that old pier in years. She was finally living an exciting story for real, and yet she didn't have a soul to tell it to! No one would ever believe her, not when even Edie hadn't.

After lying awake for what felt like an eternity, listening to her mother rise at dawn and head to open her shop, Marina showered, dressed and made her way to school.

School!

How totally, mind-numbingly dull. How could the normal humdrum of daily life in Merlington ever hold her interest again?

In spite of yesterday's storm, it was uncomfortably warm for October. The secondary school's year eight class had spent the whole day in the grip of a heat-induced boredom. Tom Fisher, a mischievous boy who rarely paid attention on the best of days, was using a magnifying glass to burn a smoky hole into his desk. Meanwhile, Daisy Baitman lavished her third coat of hot-pink nail varnish on to a tin pencil case. The combined stench was overwhelming, wafting across the room with a stink comparable to the fumes of melting plastic. Peter Featherfin sat at the back of the class and inhaled it with the greatest enthusiasm, while Edie Krill looked on in disgust.

Unmoved by any of this, Marina gazed longingly

from the window and out to sea – her thoughts lost to a new world of possibility for what could exist below the waves.

'Now, class,' called their teacher, Mrs Orr. 'Who can tell me the difference between Dover sole and lemon sole?'

How was Marina ever going to find William's father, with barely anything to go on? And what about his mother? Where would she even begin?

'Marina, what do you think?'

It was laughable really, how impossible the task before her seemed. If the biological parents for this bizarre boy existed in Merlington, surely she'd have noticed them by now?

'Marina, are you listening to me?'

Could Granny have known that there was a hint of truth to that final story she'd told? It wasn't as if boys with tentacle hair came wandering down the road very often . . .

'Marina Minnow!'

As though falling from bed, Marina came to life with a sudden jolt to find Mrs Orr towering over her desk, a look of exasperation etched on her face. Realizing she had absolutely no idea what the question was, she tugged at the depths of her memory, perfectly unaware of Edie's flailing arms and textbook on the other side of the room. They'd been learning how to fillet yesterday . . . Perhaps they were recapping that, she thought.

'Using the hole by its tail as a guide, start by dragging your knife down the centre of the fish to its head, opening the stomach?'

As the class erupted in a fit of wild laughter, Edie's palm hitting her own forehead in despair, Marina was more than certain she'd guessed wrong. Wendy Whitby had turned almost purple with glee, clutching her desk and seat in an attempt to stop herself falling to the floor.

'Quiet, class,' called Mrs Orr. 'Silence, please, control yourselves! No, Marina, that is not the answer. You haven't listened to a thing I've said all day! The question was, can anyone tell me the difference between Dover sole and lemon sole? Can you, Marina?'

'Umm . . .' It was Marina's turn to go a shade of purple, but this time from embarrassment. It was obvious she hadn't heard a word of the lesson, though luckily Wendy's incessant need to be right for once saved the day.

'I know, miss!' she called, almost feverishly. 'Lemon sole have an oval body, with a yellowish light brown skin. Dover sole are darker brown, and have a longer, narrower shape.' With the last syllable she turned her head to face Marina with a sickly-sweet smile.

'Why yes, Wendy, that's correct. Almost word for word from our textbook.'

Wendy's smile slowly shifted to one of utter smugness, teamed with an artfully raised eyebrow at Marina who was hit by a pang of fury in the centre of her heart. She was about to throw her own contemptuous glare in return, when her attention was stolen once more from the lesson.

Bobbing up and down in the window of the classroom door were the pigtails of Thea Marigold. With every leap the small girl's face was visible in the glass for just a second, but it was clear she was attempting to communicate something. Never the best at lip-reading, Marina strained closer in an attempt to decipher the words. She had barely made out the 'MAH-REE-NAH' of her own name before Mrs Orr was upon her again.

'Marina!' she shouted. 'Why exactly do you think

this lesson is not of importance to you? Is being able to correctly identify fish something you find beneath you?'

Before Marina could formulate an answer, the teacher's attention too was drawn to the small face dancing in the doorway. Storming to the entrance, she pulled the door open with such force that Thea fell into the room flat on her face. The classroom erupted once more into giggles.

'Thea Marigold!' cried Mrs Orr, sounding more and more exhausted by the minute. 'Should you not be with the rest of year seven? I do believe Mr Rybak is conducting an important lesson on identifying edible types of seaweed this afternoon.'

'Y-yes, Mrs Orr,' Thea stuttered in reply.

'Well, what are you waiting for? Run along.'

'Umm . . .'

'Come on, child, why on earth are you loitering outside my classroom?'

Marina could see the younger girl's brain working at a rate of knots, desperately seeking some kind of answer – she supposed one that would help pull Marina from class so she could confide whatever this important news was. Before either of them could land on one, Mrs Orr was pushing a dazed Thea from the room and shutting the door in her face. The pressing news she had come to deliver would need to wait a while longer.

The class returned to their lesson, as a boy named Samuel Trout was summoned to the front and tasked with drawing a diagram of the European flounder. As the depiction slowly began to look suspiciously more and more like a woman's brassiere, stifled shrieks arose within the room. But before Mrs Orr was allowed the chance to catch on, the shrieks had spilt into the corridor and grown ten times as loud. Shapes hurtled past the door and apparently out into the playground.

'What now? What is going on?' The teacher disappeared from the room and into the crowd, looking for another adult while attempting to control the rampant swarm of teenagers.

Meanwhile, Thea had slipped back into the room and charged at Marina's desk.

'You have to come to the beach! You'll never believe it, Marina!'

'Believe what? What's happening?'

'The whole school has heard about it; everyone is flipping out!'

'Heard what?'

'Is it true? Did you really row all the way over to the old pier last night?'

'How do you know that?' asked Marina. 'Edie was the only one there!' She threw a puzzled look across the classroom in her friend's direction.

'Just come, now!'

With that, Marina was up from her desk and being pulled into the throng of children fleeing the building, the entire year eight class trickling from the room behind her. Edie joined at her side.

'You told Thea about last night?' Marina whispered, as they rolled down the cliffs towards the harbour.

'Yes, only because she wanted to know where we got to after the argument. I didn't think she'd actually believe it.'

'It was the best thing I'd ever heard,' cried Thea.

'So, you believe me?' asked Marina. 'You heard about . . . You know what I found there?'

The year seven replied with an impish smile and continued to drag the girls in their confusion towards the beach.

'You'll see!' she beamed, as the other children behind them marched on their way – no idea as to what was occurring and all the more excited for it.

Opening out on to the shore, they were greeted by an enormous gaggle of children who stood ankle-deep in the surf, cooing and shrieking with laughter, pushing and shoving as they battled to get nearer to the front. What could they be looking at? A haggard old group of seagulls pecking at some poor fish that had the misfortune to wash ashore? No, why would that draw the whole school from the building? It was too big a shape to be a fish anyway, unless a shark had got lost and somehow made it to the south coast.

'Marina, you have to go and look!' said Thea.

Suddenly overcome by a feeling of great dread, Marina moved towards the mass of gulls, pushing through the children still shrieking with glee.

There, unconscious in the shallows, were the unforgettably large claws and exceptionally brilliant tentacles of her new friend, William.

CHAPTER SEVEN

Washed Up

'What the hake is that?' cried Wendy, making her way to the front of the crowd to stand beside Marina, who could only look on in horror as the foamy waves lapped at William's feet. The rest of the class gathered around tightly, having weaved their way between the legs of various adults and teachers dotted around the seafront. Crowds had begun to emerge from behind The Laughing Trout's heavy oak doors, following the trail of people spilling from the high street and past the harbour. Each had the same dumbfounded expression etched on their face.

'Gross!' jeered Tom Fisher, looking down at the grey flesh of the boy unconscious on the sand. 'It looks like something I'd sneeze into a tissue,' he said with a mixture of disgust and pride in his own mucus-making abilities.

'It looks like an old oyster that a seagull has thrown up!' laughed Samuel Trout, the two boys elbowing each other in the ribs with wide smirks.

'Don't be so horrible!' shouted Marina as she woke from her daze. She batted away the seagulls still cawing over William and sent them flying off in every direction. 'And he's not an "it", he's a "he"!' She rolled the boy on to his back and the onlookers gasped at the seemingly human face that was revealed beneath the floppy tentacles.

'I think he's brilliant!' cheered Thea, now she could see him clearly. 'And his name is *William*.'

'Oh my cod, you actually know this freak?' asked Wendy with a sneer.

'No, I don't, but Marina does. She rowed over to the old pier last night. That's where he lives, you know.'

The entire crowd on the seafront turned to face Marina in one sharp movement, like a large shoal of fish diverting from a predator. She felt their eyeballs bore into her skin, their unspoken questions and accusations scratching at her wordlessly. Wendy raised an eyebrow and broke the silence.

'As if! No one has been out to that dump in years, least of all Marina. It's just another lie; she can't help herself!'

'It's not a lie,' Edie spluttered nervously as she found the courage to come forward in her friend's defence. 'I watched her go, after we left you. She took an old boat on to the water and rowed over there. I couldn't have believed that the rest was true, though.' She looked down at the shimmering scales of the boy Marina had described last night. 'I'm sorry I doubted you.'

'That's OK,' Marina replied with an uneasy smile, taking Edie's hand. 'I'm not sure I would have believed it either.'

'I still don't,' goaded Wendy. 'She'd make up any old story to get attention. And this thing,' she stared at William with uncertainty, her eyes darting quickly from his hair to his claws, 'has to be some kind of strange, new fish . . . That, or a ropey old mannequin Marina dressed up and left here in the surf for a prank.'

'But he's breathing, Wendy,' Daisy Baitman called, pointing to William's tentacles, which seemed to hum gently with the vibrations of his quiet snores.

Marina racked her brain for a new plan of action. She hadn't anticipated having to deal with the fish-obsessed folk of Merlington so early on in her friendship with William, and now she was drawing a blank as to how best to remove him safely from the scene. The crowd was only growing thicker, and their worrying whispers had started to carry across the beach.

'Maybe we can find something smelly that might help to wake him up?' asked Thea.

'I should have something,' called Peter Featherfin as he waded through the crowd. Pulling open his overstuffed backpack he rummaged around inside. 'How about these?' he asked, holding out a large Tupperware container filled with oily anchovies which Marina took from him, the slimy fish sliding around in the see-through plastic tub like long brown tongues.

She crouched in the wet sand next to William, the cold water soaking through the fabric of her tights as the shallow waves lapped at her legs. Holding the container next to his nostrils, the translucent skin flapping with a ghostly flare upon each exhale, Marina pulled back a corner of the lid and let a waft of salty fish float into his nose.

William's eyes snapped open. He puckered his lips and slurped fourteen anchovies through the tiny gap in the tub, swallowing them in one large gulp. Slowly, he sat up, his head suddenly pounding with a low thump of delayed pain, his vision adjusting to the bright afternoon sun as the fuzzy frowns of several dozen strangers came into focus.

'Marina!' he cheered, his eyes finally landing on the face of his friend.

'See,' cried Thea. 'Of course he knows her!'

Wendy's cheeks flushed with embarrassment as she watched the impossible boy sitting before her. She turned, skulking back through the crowd and past the harbour to the high street, cursing Marina in her mind the whole way.

'William, what are you doing here?' Marina questioned urgently through gritted teeth. After staying hidden at the pier for such a long time, it seemed impossible that he would have washed up on the beach the very day after she had met him. 'We need to get you away from all these people.'

William massaged his sore head, rubbing a bruised tentacle as he tried to understand the scene in front of him. But before the dazed boy was allowed the chance to form a reply, the crowd began to erupt in excitement.

'What a beauty,' called Meredith Pike, the pharmacist from Merlington's one and only chemist, tucked away at the end of Water Lane. 'This would be a fascinating case study for my profession! There are so many fabulous medicinal properties in tentacles, and these are just superb.'

Mrs Orr appeared in the throng. 'Oh, Marina, we must have this creature for class next week. I was planning to start us on descaling very soon, and there's so much to work with here. We could learn so much!'

'Well, you'll have to fight Harold off first!' snickered Wendy's mother Winona, who had rushed down from The Laughing Trout to get the gossip for her husband at the bar. 'He'll be after one of those crab claws for an afternoon snack, I've no doubt.'

Marina looked around at the faces on the seafront. Each one stared with wide eyes of wonder at William's pincers, like hungry diners searching for the fattest lobster in the tank. He was too innocent for this fishy mob and their failure to think of anything but their bottomless stomachs. Even now, children were tugging on tentacles, prodding and poking at multicoloured scales as if William were nothing but an eel in an aquarium.

All they can see is an overgrown fish, thought Marina. *They don't know him like I do.*

She couldn't let him stay there any longer. Seizing one of his claws in her hand, she pulled the boy to his feet and pushed through the crowd. The groans of disappointment that rose all around her quickly turned to anger and outrage. She sped with her friend towards the promenade, her brisk walk turning into a full-speed run as the crowd began to follow.

CHAPTER EIGHT

Harold

*H*arold Mole was famous. Well, he was as famous as you could be in a town as small as Merlington. An imposing figure, he stood out among the masses due to his huge stature (he was as impressively tall as he was magnificently broad) and his odd but accepted obsession with fish, which was extreme, even for a town filled with fishmongers. His appetite was unrivalled, and a normal day would see him rise to a breakfast of prawn cocktail and caviar, followed by lunch of three whole lobsters with a drum of calamari. Dinner would be a feast of deep-fried fish, washed down with a pan of bouillabaisse, and the rest of the day was spent munching on sticks of crabmeat and zealously reapplying his hair ointment – a putrid-smelling tonic of fish oil that he was certain gave his lank, thinning hair a voluminous boost. The effect of this was a small gaggle of shabby seagulls who followed Harold's every waking move, now and then taking a considered dive and a quick peck at his scalp before returning to their post circling his head, confused as to their lack of a meal.

Having lived in the fishing settlement since birth (no one could quite remember how long ago that was), Harold had risen through the ranks of the Reverential Federation of Fishmongers to become the committee's Prime Warden, a position he held with the utmost pomp and devotion. Taking it upon himself to monitor the engagements of all the town's seventeen fishmongers (of which he owned six), he held a monopoly on the fresh fish caught each morning by a small army of sailors. After he had taken first preference for his flagship store, Mullet Over, followed by his other five shops, the rest of the town's fisheries were lucky to fill their freezers. None more so than Sally Minnow's tiny establishment, which Harold looked upon with the greatest contempt after his takeover bid had failed in the wake of Nigel Minnow's disappearance. He had made it his personal mission ever since to drive her out of business, so that she might learn her lesson. There was no one who could hold a grudge quite like Harold.

After a strangely troubled night's sleep, the morning of 28 October had been much like any other for Harold Mole. He'd woken to his normal pint of prawn cocktail and caviar before heading downstairs to open the Mullet Over in time for the early deliveries, its red-and-white canopy gleaming from the previous evening's rainfall.

Jasper Jenkins had brought by an entire crate of live crabs that Harold bought up in a flash, displaying them proudly in the shop's enormous front window with a sign marked: *£12.99, 2 for £23.50*. Goldie Harrison had shuffled in on her morning walk and demanded to buy some of the beautifully fresh plaice that he was wrapping behind the counter, refusing to budge as always when he told her it was already on order for The Laughing Trout.

Yes, Harold's day had gone much like any other, until the silence of a quiet Friday afternoon was broken by the unpleasant buzz of the shop telephone bursting into life.

'Yes,' bellowed Harold, as he picked up the olive-coloured receiver. He hated speaking on the phone and after tucking the mouthpiece between his shoulder and stubbly chin, he anxiously squeezed a slimy dollop of fish oil into his palm and ran it furiously through his greasy locks. A blob of fat dripped down his cheek and fell on to the pristine white apron he wore, the Mullet Over logo embroidered at the centre of his chest.

'Harold? It's me,' answered Walter Whitby, the grisly landlord of The Laughing Trout. Harold had been expecting him to pick up his order for the Catch of the Day hours ago.

'What time do you call this? I've got three kilos of fish here that's not getting any fresher! That old bat Goldie Harrison gave me a good offer this morning too, but, no, I'm holding it for Walter, I told her. Where the haddock have you been?'

Harold greeted the postman with a curt nod as he

entered the store and left several soggy letters on the counter, still dripping inside their glass bottles.

'Sorry, Harold, it's all been kickin' off!' Walter panted. 'Have you not heard what's going on down the beach? I thought you'd be over 'ere by now.'

'What do you mean?' replied Harold, eyeing a rundown seagull that had wandered through the doorway as the postman left the store. He plonked a paper hat back on his head and reached for the broom that lay beside the storeroom entrance . . . 'What's happening at the beach?'

'The whole town's come down 'ere – something washed up on the shore overnight, knocked out cold!'

'What do you mean, "something"?'

'Well, some*one*, maybe, none of us are sure,' Walter said.

'Hardly front-page news, now, is it? Plenty of folks are found asleep on the sand after a heavy night at The Laughing Trout. I'll bet he's been there for hours, but nobody's found the layabout 'til now.'

Harold edged out from behind the long counter, which was stuffed full of the most luxurious display of seafood. He stretched the phone cord as he moved forward, all the time eyeballing the lone seagull as it shifted its way further into the room with craving and curiosity.

'It's not like that,' continued Walter. 'It . . . I mean, he, weren't even in the pub – 'e's just a boy, barely a teenager, I reckon. Not only that, I'm not even sure that 'e's a boy. He's . . .'

With a great crash Harold leapt across the room, slamming his broom into the ground as the seagull took flight just in time and began circling the tentacle-shaped ceiling light that hung over the store with eight glowing, fluorescent bulbs. Before the fishmonger had a moment to collect himself, the bird swept down and took a painful chunk from his greasy scalp.

'Ow, blooming hake!' cried Harold. 'You flapping parasite! The bleeding thing's made me bleed!'

'Harold? Harold!' came the muffled voice still bleating from the plastic phone receiver abandoned on the floor, which was slowly springing back across the polished white tiles to its wall mount. Having successfully shooed the hungry gull from the door-way, Harold returned to the counter and took up the phone again in one hand, rubbing his scalp with the other.

'I'm here, I'm here, flaming vultures . . .'

'Harold, did you 'ear me? Did you 'ear what I said?' pleaded Walter.

'Yeah, yeah, some kid has washed up on the beach. It's not like you're going to lose your pub licence over it, mate. What's all the fuss about?'

'No, Harold, you ain't listening. He wasn't just a boy – 'e, this sounds insane, 'e was . . . a fish!'

Stunned into silence, Harold sat back on to his worktable with a squelch, his large buttocks crushing a pile of prawns that virtually burst from their shells, their black eyes bulging under the impressive weight.

'. . . Y-y-you what?'

'A fish, Harold! More fish than boy, maybe. He had tentacles for hair, long greasy things, an' 'e was covered in scales . . . with these great big pincers! Crab ones, instead of 'ands!'

The blood drained from Harold's face in an instant as Walter Whitby continued to blather away, unaware of the effect of his words.

'. . . Swear the wife took a shine to him – says he was cute! Honestly, cute? Total freak, if you ask—'

'Where is he now?' interrupted Harold with a splutter. 'The – fish thing, the tentacle boy . . . where did he go?'

'The Minnow girl. The whole school came down when they heard what was goin' on and she seemed t'know him. When 'e finally came to she ran off with him somewhere, everyone chasing after . . . Had to grab hold of Winona, she wanted to—'

The phone crashed to the floor with a bang once again as Harold pulled off his paper hat and stormed from the counter, spoilt prawns dropping from the seat of his trousers like squashed grey slugs and leaving a trail of gunk in his wake.

He flipped over a sign in the window that read *Back in 10 Minutes*, and the door was almost pulled from its hinges as he burst into the afternoon sun with a face like thunder.

CHAPTER NINE
The Last to Hear

Sally Minnow's fishmonger's was five doors down, at the harbour end of the high street, and the last in a line of coveted shops that backed directly on to the docks. As the road faded into beach beside The Laughing Trout, the rest of the town's fisheries turned from the promenade and ran along Water Lane as it curled into the town, away from the seafront.

Minnow's was a tiny, tattered establishment that

had been run by the family for generations. On the large front window, the letters of their modest surname were stencilled in metallic gold, which flaked softly like crumbling autumn leaves. Following her husband's disappearance and presumed death, Sally had grown fiercely protective of the faltering fishmonger's legacy. The fact that Minnow's had the bad luck to find itself positioned next door to one of Harold Mole's five other stores, No Plaice Like Home, meant a great deal of her energy was spent fighting off his relentless plans of expansion. In his eyes, Minnow's was nothing more than a waste of good retail space – its location prime as one of the few fisheries in town with harbour access directly outside the storeroom.

A spindly woman, with wiry blonde hair and kind hazel eyes, Marina's mother was as nice a person as you could hope to meet – but when it came to her family, she would not hear a bad word. It was this very fire that would find her defending Marina's tall tales at every turn. It spurred on the tiresome journey to her mother-in-law's nursing home on the cliffs week in week out, and fuelled the same loyalty that saw her pour her heart, soul and savings into her family's struggling shop.

Sally stood alone behind the counter like any other Friday afternoon, deftly descaling a skinny silver herring before reaching for a pair of pliers to begin deboning its flesh. Her lame offering of whitebait and some meagre-looking mussels barely filled the tiny freezer, but her heart gave a skip at the sound of the shop door dinging as it opened. *A customer!* Her joy was short-lived, though, as Harold Mole sidestepped awkwardly through the entrance, his huge frame blotting out the sun and casting an ominous square shadow across the room.

'For the last time, Harold, I'm not selling,' Sally hissed, her good mood disappearing with the thud of a steel anchor. 'You can save your breath, please, as it's not going to happen. I'll go out of business before you get your greasy mitts on Minnow's!'

'Believe it or not, I haven't come to destroy your spirit today,' spat Harold with a sneer. 'You know why I'm here, so just tell me where it is.'

'Tell you where what is, exactly?'

'Don't play dumb, Sally. The whole town saw your darling daughter run off with it. Always interfering, aren't you? Why your family can't just leave things alone I don't know.'

'Marina ran off with what?' Sally demanded, her heart beginning to race in time with her working mind. What could that girl have got herself into now? She knew not to take Harold Mole's word for it, but Sally couldn't help worrying when it came to Marina and her overactive imagination.

'You don't know?' spluttered Harold, aghast. 'You don't even know what your own child gets up to! I should've guessed. I wouldn't care either, in all honesty, but when she's dragging the town's reputation into question and mixing with monstrosities like that, it becomes *my* problem.'

'Harold, what on earth are you talking about?'

'Some half-fish, tentacle-haired freak show,' he continued, 'has washed up on the beach and was last seen cavorting around town with your delinquent girl Marina.'

Harold folded his arms in a show of impatience, and Sally felt the full weight of her worry leave her body with a *whoosh*. She doubled over in laughter, screeching with glee at the absurdity.

'You've clearly inhaled too much fish oil, Harold; you've finally lost the plot!' she cried with delight. 'If you honestly believe that load of old claptrap, you're thoroughly mad.'

'Too right I'm mad! If your daughter turns this town into a laughing stock, you'll have me to answer to, I promise you that.'

'Go on, Harold, tell me another one. I needed a good laugh today!'

'You won't be laughing once Merlington becomes a circus,' he jeered, grinding his teeth. 'You want to be famous, is that it? You want to try and steal my business? I bet you fancy yourself as the next Prime Warden of the Reverential Federation of Fishmongers!'

Losing interest in Harold's nonsense, Sally wiped her eyes with a sigh, and turned her attention to a bucket of old fish in need of disposal.

'Yes, you're exactly right. I model myself on you,' she said sarcastically, rolling her eyes as she tried to restore a straight face. 'Didn't you know that you're my idol, Harold?'

'If your husband could see what a mess you've made of things, I dare say he'd sail out into the wintery night all over again!' Harold mocked cruelly, looking up at the Minnow family name which hung behind the frostbitten counter in faded lettering.

The heartless comment forced Sally to suddenly

shrink backwards in pain, her hand on her chest. 'Get out, *now*!'

Huffing with frustration, Harold pulled the shop door open with an unsuitably delicate ding. 'You don't have to tell me twice. If that overgrown fish *thing* shows up, you let me know without fail.'

'Just go,' Sally demanded. 'There are no tentacle boys here, I promise you that!'

Harold lurched out into the street, muttering obscenities under his breath as the door crashed shut behind him. Sally perched on the edge of the counter, winded by Harold's cruel jibe until a sigh of relief finally swelled inside of her. She let herself relax, the absurdity of his story dawning on her.

Returning to her bucket of offal and squatting under its weight, she pigeon-walked her way around the counter and moved into the storeroom. She squinted in the dark as she pulled the bucket across the floor and out on to the small dock which catered to the handful of fishermen still visiting her with their sad offerings.

She began to shovel the foul-smelling mix of fish heads, guts and bones from her bucket and into the water, tiny crabs snapping at the air as chunks sank past their pincers. While gulls cawed in the sky and dived in their direction, Sally couldn't help but wonder how different life might have been if her husband were still around. Since when had she cared so much about fish? Was she really slogging her own guts out every day of the week just to spite Harold Mole? This town was totally bonkers, and she'd had bigger plans for her life before she'd found herself embroiled in a battle over brill and bream. There was no chance of that now, with an elderly mother-in-law to visit at the home and Marina daydreaming her way through school. Had her daughter been right all along? Was Merlington actually as dull as she'd always said?

Sally turned back into the storeroom and dropped the empty bucket at her feet with a shriek. Marina's face had suddenly appeared through the gloom.

As the young girl moved out from her hiding place behind the rusting industrial freezer and walked slowly into the light, Sally was surprised to notice that she held in her hand the claw of a boy with the most peculiar-looking hair.

CHAPTER TEN

A New Friend

Billy Bass had travelled well in his short, tumultuous life. 'Big Mouth' to those who knew him well, he'd come into this world one Tuesday morning, assembled by the finest manufacturers in the whole of Irving, Texas. Then, packed into a wooden crate alongside dozens of his identical brothers, all mounted on similar plaques and cushioned by a blanket of polystyrene chips, he was transported across the country and delivered to a hardware store on New York's lower east side. There, he was unboxed and hung on a set of metal prongs. The very next morning and for the tidy sum of $29.95, he could be yours, batteries not included.

For weeks he gathered dust, staring blankly through his plastic shell and across the aisle at a wall display of nails, nuts and bolts, wondering where life would take him and to what purpose. Finally, one February morning, the wind off the Hudson River blew Larry Wilson through the front doors of the store and on to aisle five in search of a wrench. Instead, Larry found himself captivated by Billy's crummy charm and immediately threw thirty dollars on to the counter before mounting the mechanical fish to the wall of his bar. Patrons of Wilson's were delighted when they popped to the loo, pushing down 'Big Mouth' Billy's button as he broke into song, twisting his rubber face away from the wall and lip-synching to the great Johnny Cash.

When Larry's bartending dream came to a sudden end after one too many missed tax returns, Wilson's closed for good and Billy was sent to the nearby ninety-nine cents store. The following summer,

Françoise Desjardins, on her holidays from Brittany, wandered into the shop on the corner of Grand and Jackson and saved Billy from a date with the skip. Stowing him in her luggage and flying him back across the Atlantic, she found him a new home on the bathroom wall of her small-town bistro. It was there Billy learnt the joys of French cuisine, and grew very fond of his charming new mistress. Sadly, Françoise fell afoul of her thirty-a-day cigarette habit, passing away with a final puff and leaving the bistro to her son Benoît. A modern man, he shut up shop and turned the restaurant into an internet cafe, placing 'Big Mouth' Billy on an auction website overnight. It was there that a collector of turn-of-the-century tat named Nigel Minnow spotted the bass-baritone, snapping him up for €7.40, plus postage.

Now, Billy hung on the wall of the modest Merlington fishmonger's known as Minnow's, an object of extreme fascination to William, the boy with scales. He stared up at the rubber bass with the greatest interest, before pushing the big red button with his oversized claw for the sixth time, and as Billy broke out into a tinny rendition of 'Walk the Line' William wondered how this immortal fish had come to be nailed on the wall, forever singing the blues.

'Marina,' rasped Sally in a hushed but frantic whisper, pulling her daughter behind the cracked counter. 'I don't know what you could have been thinking! Bringing this creature here, do you know what you've done?'

'I did exactly what you would have done, Mum. I helped someone in need. Isn't that the kind of thing you always taught me to do? To look out for those in trouble, not to judge a person on appearance . . .' She looked up at her mother with a pair of large doe eyes. 'To be more like Dad.'

Marina knew that she had her mother cornered. Sally had always taught her daughter to see the good in people, a trait which she was proud to possess. (Though she drew a line at trying to find any good in Wendy Whitby!)

'He's a boy, not a creature. And you didn't see him in that shack, Mum. He was so alone, left there for who knows how long with nothing to do but swim about in the darkness and read old sardine tins!'

'Sardine tins?' said her mother with a quizzical look.

'And what was I supposed to do? I couldn't just leave him on the beach to be gawped at. He'd have been sent off to some horrible doctors' lab for experiments or served up for lunch in The Laughing Trout, if he hadn't been hacked to death by those mangy seagulls first!'

Sally Minnow considered this as she took in the strange boy standing in her shop for the umpteenth time. His bizarre tentacles were swaying in time with Billy Bass, and she stared in astonishment at the explosion of colour which rippled across his scaly back under the harsh tube lighting. How could this boy exist? How was it even possible? Had he really been living in that shack out at sea, with the whole town none the wiser, all of this time?

'WILL-EE-UM?' Sally bellowed over yet another rendition of Johnny Cash. William leapt to attention with a jolt of surprise. 'I AM SAH-LEE, MAH-REE-NA'S MUH-MEE.'

'Mum!' cried Marina. 'He can speak English.'

'Oh, I'm sorry, excuse me.' She frowned at her daughter. 'How was I supposed to know?'

'Sardine tins,' Marina scolded, shaking her head with embarrassment. 'William, this is my mum. You can trust her. We're going to look after you now!'

Sally cleared her throat loudly, but Marina ignored her, knowing it was already far too late to revoke the offer.

'That's really nice,' said William, smiling. 'Thank you. Both of you.' He joined them by the counter, before rubbing an amber claw on the glass in front. Peering through the condensation, he spied a sad heap of mussels swimming about in the melting slush.

'Yes, of course we'll help you,' conceded Sally. 'I can't imagine what you've been through.'

William looked around the sad fishmonger's, its crooked sign hanging high on the wall opposite a poster of a caricature fish. The cartoon cod shared a bath with a fat golden chip, and poured a bottle of brown vinegar down on their heads. William's eyes found their way to Sally's work counter, where her descaled herring was now sweating from the humidity. His eyes widened with horror at the cold, metallic instruments, and a shiver ran down his spine which caused every one of his own scales to ripple with nausea.

'Life has definitely become a little weirder since I met Marina,' he gulped.

Sally couldn't help thinking that her own definition of weird would pale in comparison to that of this already peculiar boy.

'Why don't you tell us, William?' she offered. 'Start from the very beginning.'

CHAPTER ELEVEN

William's Story

William shook his tentacle hair as he considered where the beginning of the story would be, before taking one claw in the other and perching delicately on the edge of the hard counter.

'Um, well, after I helped Marina steer her boat back to shore,' he started, 'I sneaked away along the seabed when that spotty red bug girl came running down the beach.'

'Bug girl?' interrupted Sally, already confused.

'Edie's umbrella,' replied Marina impatiently. 'Go on, William,' she encouraged.

'Like I said, after you left, I headed back along the sea floor towards the pier, but the water started to get too rough even for me to make it home safely. Since no one was around, I thought it best to hide from the storm among the weeds and the sand while I waited for the weather to relax a little. I dug a small hole in the seabed so I could nestle down for the night, but accidentally sat on a sleeping lemon sole . . .'

'Lemon sole!' cried Marina with delight. 'You won't have noticed it due to its dark brown skin, which helps to camouflage it against the sand.'

'Actually, lemon sole are a lighter, more yellow shade of brown,' replied William matter-of-factly.

'Yes, Marina, it's Dover sole that are dark brown,' corrected her mother. 'Honestly, what are they teaching you at that school? Everybody knows that!'

'As I keep hearing,' said Marina, blushing.

'Anyway,' continued William, taking no notice of his new friend's reddening cheeks. 'After I untangled a clump of seaweed for a blanket, I accidentally fell asleep as my little ditch was so comfy. I must have been out for a few hours, because by the time I woke up the water was as still as the moonlight. I thought I should head home before sunrise, in case anybody spotted me climbing on to the pier, but then I noticed a shadow on the surface of the sea and heard the faint sound of an engine. Normally I would steer clear of any boats, or I'd quickly head back to the shack as they never want to come near there. But then I thought it might be you, Marina, coming to see me again. So, I swam after it.

'There was no sound except for the waves breaking on the shore, and no other movement but the flashing light of a red buoy above me. When the boat's engine turned off, the silence was really creepy. I had no idea what you would be doing outside the harbour so late, and I really wanted to see you, so I swam upwards to find out. But the moment I broke through the surface an object came hurtling over the side of the boat, cracked me on the head, and that's the last thing I knew before I woke up on the warm beach covered in seagulls and dozens of goggling children.'

William finished his story with a satisfied nod, hopping down from the counter. Marina scratched her head in bewilderment. She hated to admit it, even to herself, but this turn of events had her well and truly stumped.

'Well, it definitely wasn't me out on a boat in the middle of the night . . .'

'I should flipping well hope not!' shrieked her mother, wringing her hands at the thought. Sally too was at a loss. What could someone have been dumping in the sea, in the early hours of the morning, that was large enough to knock out this curious creature?

Marina let out a yelp of excitement.

'Oh, Mum! I remember now. I woke up in the middle of the night, some time around three o'clock. I didn't sleep well, because I was too excited, and I heard a speedboat! In the distance. I can remember it so clearly. The sound carried right through my bedroom window.'

'You heard a boat from our house?' Sally asked. 'The fishermen don't work on that side of the harbour, and the storm would've only just petered out around that time. What on earth could they have been doing?'

'Getting rid of something?' Marina considered. 'Throwing it into the sea. Maybe something they don't want anyone to know about?' Her mind was racing. 'Unlucky for them, they knocked William out in the process.'

'I was lucky they didn't squash one of my tentacles!' he added with a huff, turning back to 'Big Mouth' Billy's plaque and massaging a patch of his rubbery scalp with his claw.

'William, can you remember anything about what it was that hit you?' asked Marina. 'Anything at all?'

'I'm afraid not. I just remember waking up on that beach with one hell of a bad headache.'

'Then we *have* to find out what it was. Tomorrow morning we'll go snorkelling in the bay and see what we can find. Whatever's down there could be the key to your history!'

'Hold your seahorses,' Sally stressed with increasing concern. 'We don't know anything about this person, what they threw into the sea, or even if they're connected to William in the first place. Most likely it's a total coincidence.'

'There's something fishy going on, Mum, and we have to get to the bottom of it!' cheered Marina, addressing her troops as if it were the eve of battle. 'William, can you tell us anything more about the fisherman that first brought you to the pier? I'm sure he must be someone who lives in Merlington.'

William racked his brain. The fisherman he called Father was the kindest man he'd ever met. He was the *only* man he'd ever met! He'd tried to decorate his happily murky home with framed pictures and blankets. He had taught him how to walk and talk, and encouraged his reading by bringing along the earliest tins that had started the boy's rusty, metallic library. But it had been so long since his last visit, and now William was forced to fill his endless days with fishing, swimming and staying far out of the sight of the strange folk that walked on dry land – no matter how lonely he was. The fisherman had always said that it wasn't safe for him to be seen . . .

'Marina,' interrupted Sally. 'Maybe now is not the time for this.'

'But, Mum, we have to find out what's really going on – starting with this mysterious midnight motorboat. It might give us the answer William has been looking for all of these years! It's *too* much of a coincidence . . .'

'You may well be right about that, but perhaps it's best if we continue this discussion . . . later?' offered her mother, twisting her head slowly in the direction of Minnow's front window with widened eyes.

Marina had noticed the room get darker all of a sudden. But instead of finding that a fleet of grey clouds was blotting the late afternoon sky, she discovered that the entire glass storefront of the fishmonger's was filled with the silent, ogling faces of Merlington's curious inhabitants. As their eyes settled on William when he finally wandered into view, they exploded to life like a squad of startled squid. Screaming and cheering as they threw questions at the glass like ink.

'WHAT IS IT, SALLY?'

'WHERE DID YOU FIND IT?'

'HOW FANTASTIC!'

'DOES IT WORK HERE NOW?'

'IS IT WEARING A COSTUME?'

'HOW MUCH FOR ONE OF THOSE TASTY-LOOKING CLAWS?'

'WILL YOU PRE-FILLET FOR ME?'

'I REALLY FANCIED SOME CALAMARI TONIGHT!'

CHAPTER TWELVE

Sashimi

Marina stood frozen on the spot, for once in her life unable to speak, while William slammed down Billy Bass's red button and dropped to the floor, humming along to 'Ring of Fire'. Sally, after a moment of motionless panic, eased herself slowly towards the windows and, plastering an enormous fake smile across her face, began to gently lower the metal blinds, to huge shouts of anger from the swelling crowd outside.

The evening drew in as they waited for the noise from the baiting mob to die down, their cries carrying along the high street and across the harbour. A sense of foreboding hung over the shop. Sally sat on a stool and contemplated their next move, and Marina tried to push away the hunger now possessing her and increasing in intensity by the second. Her stomach let out a particularly loud growl that ripped through the room and caused William to yelp in surprise.

'I seriously need something to eat,' she moaned, clutching her stomach and starting to pace the room. 'I've not had anything since lunch.'

'Well,' barked her mother irritably. 'Unless you want to go out and pick something up from the shop, we don't have anything.'

Marina's stomach churned again as she plonked back on to the cold floor tiles and resigned herself to a few more hours of misery.

'I'm pretty sure that I can smell something tasty,' chimed William. Since he had been balled up in the corner until then, anxiously wringing his tentacles, the sudden declaration startled both of the Minnows.

'Oh,' said Sally in understanding. 'That will

probably be the salmon fillets I was going to bring home for dinner. You've quite the powerful nose!'

'Mum, that's great!' Marina cheered. 'A fisherman sold you some salmon today?'

'No, I bought it from Shrimpy's over the road,' she admitted. 'Harold Mole still has most of the fishermen refusing to visit us. After sixteen other shops have bought from them first, I'm lucky if I see a few pollock. Anyway, we can't eat that until we're home – I don't have a proper kitchen here to cook it.'

'Cook it? Bleurgh!' cried William, leaping from the floor and shooting into the storage room. Sally and Marina flew after him just in time to see the boy spring through the back door and dive from the small jetty, disappearing head first into the murky harbour waters.

Completely bemused, Marina and her mother ran to the exit and peered over the edge. As they leant closer, as close as they would dare, squinting deeper and deeper into the muddy pool, William burst from the surface like a firework without warning and landed between them, showering the pair in great dirty sploshes. Shaking his wet tentacle hair like a shaggy dog, he marched triumphantly back through to the front of the shop cradling a great bundle of green seaweed in his arms.

'Mrs Minnow, would you please bring me the salmon you mentioned?'

Puzzled, Sally obliged and went to fetch four beautifully filleted pieces of fish from the fridge, bound delicately in a thin sheet of brown paper that was patterned with the familiar prawn logo of Shrimpy's fishmonger. As Sally unwrapped the package on the counter, William dried a clump of seaweed and flattened it on the worktop. Taking up his claws, he ran the blades of his pincers against each other with a fierce purpose and the sound of sharpening steel. Satisfied with his freshly whetted tools, William took the first piece of salmon and threw it high above his head. Before it could even fall beneath his eye level, he had skimmed a claw through the air, pinceing and pinching in a blur of activity, as twelve perfectly chopped pieces of finely sliced salmon landed delicately on the bed of seaweed with a light bounce.

'Whoa,' mouthed Marina, as she slumped against the wall in awe and slid to the ground in a pile.

'Go ahead,' encouraged William with enthusiasm. 'Eat!'

'Eat it? What, raw?' Marina recoiled, her tongue lurching from the corner of her lips in disgust, as though it were attempting to pack up its bags and leave her mouth for good out of sheer protest.

'Well, I couldn't let you ruin it by cooking it!'

'Oh, yes,' laughed her mother in realization. 'This is sashimi, isn't it? I've heard of this, it's a Japanese delicacy.'

'Sashimi?' asked William, confused.

'Never mind,' replied Sally, scooping up a piece of fish in her hands. It smelt divine, fresh and light, and her mouth was suddenly filled with saliva and anticipation. She popped it between her lips and the fragile fish melted on her tongue.

'Oh, William,' she cooed. 'It's absolutely delicious. I would never have thought to try something like this myself in a million years. Marina, eat your dinner and don't be so rude!'

Marina lifted herself from the floor with a groan as her mother popped another piece of sashimi into her mouth. Marina's stomach grumbled with a keen hunger she could no longer ignore, and she approached the counter and the plate of fleshy orange fish.

Here goes nothing, she thought, picking up a piece between her fingertips and nipping it into her mouth, which she held open as widely as her lips would allow (which was not very wide at all). She pinched her nose as she chewed, but it tasted . . . OK! Better than OK. The fish was as fresh as anything Marina had eaten, and the salty, crisp seaweed was the perfect accompaniment.

'Mum, this is delicious! William, you're a culinary genius!' she cried.

William blushed at the praise, if you could call it blushing. His translucent, ghostly skin turned a slightly more opaque kind of grey, as Marina and her mum huddled over their dinner and stuffed their beaming faces with delight.

'William, where on earth did you learn to make such tasty food?' Sally asked through a mouthful of salmon. She covered her lips with a hand in embarrassment.

'There isn't much to do back home, so dinner time is by far my favourite part of the day. I've been practising for years!' William tossed another two salmon fillets into the air, slicing them with precision, before catching the fourth and final fillet in his mouth and swallowing it in one big gulp.

Once darkness had embraced the streets outside and they were certain the townsfolk's boredom would have finally overcome their curiosity, at least for this evening, Sally, Marina and William sneaked from the fishmonger's and out into the night. They crept along the silent high street away from the harbour, and would have been unseen, if not for a pair of large and angry eyes surveying them with a quiet fury from the dark windows of the Mullet Over.

CHAPTER THIRTEEN

A Bed in a Bath

As the narrow streets of Merlington weaved away from the seafront, criss-crossing in tight spirals that wound up the cliffs, the smells of salt and fish faded away with the breeze. The landscape of wooden wharfs and shining shopfronts melted into pastel houses with weathered paint and timber decking, their terracotta chimneys billowing white smoke from the top of slanted roofs.

The crooked Minnow house was on a quiet street named Porter Lane, crushed between two overgrown trees whose sprawling roots threatened to break through the walls at the slowest of paces. William's eyes lit up at the cosy home as he entered, taking in the warming yellow walls and soft shaggy carpet of the living room. The house was bursting with memories, from the dozens of seashells collected at the beach one summer now glued on the wooden mantelpiece, to the great dark stain on the kitchen curtains from Marina's failed attempt to make a Mississippi Mud Pie, with mud.

'Marina, will you sort William out with a bed in the bathroom? I guess he'll have to be comfortable there, at least for tonight.'

'Mum,' asked Marina tentatively, catching her grandmother's eye from the small picture frame that hung above the kitchen table. A single thought had troubled her ever since it had sprung from the depths of her memory in the middle of the night. 'Did Granny Minnow ever tell you a story? One that might now feel a bit familiar?'

'Marina, I don't think I can handle any more tales tonight,' Sally sighed, only half listening through her exhaustion. 'Can we please just go to bed?'

Well, that settled that. If she *had* been told the same story of the fisherman's strange catch that was now so vivid at the forefront of Marina's brain, her mother would surely have made the same connection. Instead, she seemed blissfully unaware.

'OK, never mind. Sleep tight, Mum.'

'Goodnight, my darling,' smiled Sally. 'Everything will work out fine, I promise.'

Sally retired to her bedroom, immediately climbing in between her comfortable cotton sheets and pulling a cat's-eye sleeping mask over her own as she allowed tiredness to wash over her.

On the other side of the house Marina ran the bath, waiting until the water flowed lukewarm before plugging the drain, then filling the tub a few centimetres and shutting off the tap. She ran her fingers back and forth through the tepid water.

'How's that?' she asked.

'Great,' said William, watching quizzically from the doorway and clearly perplexed by how the walls of such a tiny house could hold so much liquid. 'I only like it a little bit damp. Do you have any salt?'

'Salt?'

'Well, the pier gets pretty salty from all the seawater . . .'

'Oh, of course!' cried Marina. She ran to the kitchen, rummaging through the cupboards but finding nothing useful except for a half-empty bottle of fish sauce. 'How can we not have any salt?' she whined. She realized that they'd barely eaten anything except takeaway for the last few months. Mum had been working so hard to get the shop on its feet again . . .

Dashing back to the bathroom she shook the bottle of fish sauce into the tub, the water turning a translucent golden brown.

'I hope this will do,' she said, looking up at William with apologetic eyes, and swilling the water with a metal whisk.

'It looks perfect!' he cried with genuine enthusiasm. 'I love my pier but it can get pretty cold sometimes, and there's one big lump in my piles of nets that I can't ever seem to smooth out.'

'Well, that could be all of the tin cans underneath,' giggled Marina. 'Honestly, William, I don't know how you managed out there for so long on your own. I'd have gone mad from boredom.'

'It's not all that bad. I've my own, endless swimming pool right outside the window, and all the fish that I could ever want to eat. Sometimes, when the waves get really choppy, I close my eyes and pretend I'm on a rollercoaster, the shack sways so wildly on its stilts.'

'You know about rollercoasters?'

William smiled wistfully. 'There's a picture of one on the side of a fizzy drink can in my collection. If I can find two more we could exchange them for half-priced entry!'

Marina laughed out loud. 'But what about friends?' she asked, noticing William's smile drop slightly downwards at this and immediately regretting the question.

'I'd always hoped that I'd visit land someday, and would have loved to meet a few people my own age,' he sighed. 'But my father warned me that it wasn't safe yet. When he didn't come back, I had to stay put, in case I missed his next visit.'

'What do you mean, "safe yet"?' Marina wondered.

'I don't really know; he was probably just being cautious. I can't see what all the worry was about, everyone I've met so far has been lovely!' he beamed, missing Marina's sceptical look as she thought back to the hungry crowd on the beach.

'Well, I'm glad you're here, William,' she grinned. 'Before I met you my life was just one made-up story after another. My dad always loved it when we told each other stories, but everyone else in this town thinks I'm a troublemaker. With you, I'm finally having a real adventure.'

'Will you tell me one of your stories?' asked William, climbing into the bath. 'Please?'

'Would you like that?'

'Oh, yes, very much,' he sighed, peering up from his porcelain bed as he swirled his scaly toes in the salty water.

'OK, then, I'd love to!' Marina smiled widely. The last person who had actually *asked* to hear one of her stories was Granny Minnow . . .

She looked around the bathroom for inspiration and her eyes landed on the garish shower curtain tucked behind the towel rail. She allowed its pattern of green frogs to play with her eyes and her imagination.

'Once upon a time, there was a gardener,' she began, 'a young man who lived for his afternoons pruning flowers, pulling weeds and planting bulbs.

One day, at the bottom of his yard, where a gentle stream ran through the divide between his home and the woodland behind, the gardener sat taking clippings from a begonia bush. Just as he was considering fetching a glass of lemonade, he heard a peculiar noise coming from the reeds. Leaning towards the stream, craning his neck as far as possible, he thought it sounded very much like Tchaikovsky's famous violin concerto. Baffled, he lay on his front and reached towards the noise, parting the reeds with his fingers. There in the water sat a group of seven frogs, now frozen in silence as the gardener took them in.

'Could it have been real? Days went by and he thought of nothing but the frog chorus at the bottom of his garden. It seemed impossible, but every afternoon without fail those dulcet tones rose from the reeds, only to cease when he tried to catch the performers in action. Resolving to prove his own sanity, the young man bought a video camera and crawled into the undergrowth. And then he waited. Hours went by, until finally the frogs emerged as the evening took shape. It was then he caught on film their most sublime rendition of Vivaldi's "Four Seasons", croaked to pitch-perfection.

'Well, the reaction was astounding. The video made the local news and the entire village was in awe of this amphibian choir. A concert was booked at the town hall for the very next evening at the mayor's special request, and the frog chorus were scooped up from their stream and delivered to the venue like royalty, bass notes and tenor croaks emitting from their box the whole way. After a quick pep talk from the gardener, he placed the chorus on a small desk on stage where a large brass megaphone was fixed to the front. The frogs lined up for their adoring audience who were on the edges of their seats . . .

'And they waited. Five, fifteen, thirty minutes passed, and the frogs remained silent, without so much as a scale or arpeggio. An hour went by. "He's a liar," the audience cried. Two hours. "That flipping gardener faked the video!" In a fury the spectators surged from the hall and into the night, cursing the whole way. The gardener, defeated, the most humiliated man in town, crumpled to the floor of the empty room in disgrace. It was only then that a huge croak emitted from the largest of the frogs and at once, all seven of them joined together for the delicate first notes of Beethoven's Symphony No. 7. And the gardener, forgetting his humiliation, was overcome by gratitude, and privilege, at witnessing this private recital.

'How was that, William?'

Marina looked down at the sleeping boy from the sea, his tentacles purring in time with the rise and fall of his breathing chest.

CHAPTER FOURTEEN

The New Look

On a typical Saturday morning, Marina could easily have slept as late as eleven o'clock before finding the energy to leave her bed. She would doze and dream, waking just long enough to remember it was the weekend, before pushing her face back into her squidgy white pillow with glee. She'd toss and turn and crawl under the duvet to block out the light teasing through the curtains, stretching her limbs with a satisfying tingle.

But this was no typical Saturday.

Today the hands of Marina's bedside clock had barely ticked past seven before she'd thrown off the duvet, hurled herself from bed and crashed into the bathroom with a skid on the smooth floor.

'William?' she called, finding the bath empty. In a sudden panic, she darted through the small house, doubt beginning to flood her thoughts. Where could he have got to? Had he ever really been here at all? It seemed too exciting an adventure to have been true, more likely one of her own peculiar tales which she had fallen into in a dream...

Crying his name, Marina fell through the living-room door, to finally find her strange new friend hunched over the slapdash shell-covered fireplace.

'Good morning, Marina. Sorry, I didn't want to wake you up.'

'That's OK!' she coughed in relief, inhaling the feathery shag pile rug. 'I couldn't have slept any longer if I tried. What have you got there?'

William looked down at the frame he held in his claws. A man and a woman, both looking young enough to be teenagers, smiled up at him. The woman wore a white lace gown and a veil trimmed with glossy oyster pearls. In her arms she cradled a delicate bouquet of orange starfish, dried sponges and multicoloured sea anemones.

'That's my parents on their wedding day,' said Marina, joining him. 'See? Do you recognize my mum?'

William stared blankly at her.

'Don't worry, I wouldn't either. They both look so young. This is pretty much how I remember my dad, though – how he looks in these pictures. He was much older by the time he disappeared, but I was only six. I just get flashes of him then, mostly in dreams...'

William looked down at the handsome man. He wore a very smart suit and his short, frizzy hair was parted on one side. From his buttonhole flowed a long stalk of green seaweed. He beamed with happiness.

'That gives me an idea!' cried Marina, snatching the frame and placing it back on the mantelpiece. 'We could find you some clothes to wear in Dad's wardrobe. We've kept all his old stuff, just as he left it. It could help you to blend in a little better,' she said, surveying his glistening scales with a furrowed brow.

She dragged him by the claw to her mother's bedroom, and together they rummaged through the closet of musty clothes as Marina pulled shirts, trousers, braces and brogues from the depths, along with a cloud of dust and a family of fluttering moths.

'Some of this will probably be way too big, but we can make do.'

'What're these meant to be?' asked William, holding up some adult-sized rubber fishing waders before accidentally snapping the shoulder strap in half with his claw.

'They're waterproof wellies that you wear right up to your chest! I'm not sure they'd stay up now, though. How about . . . these?'

Marina tossed a bundle of clothes on to the bed and then helped to pull a cream cable-knit jumper over William's head, which she paired with some beige corduroy trousers.

'There,' beamed Marina, surveying her work. 'They're a little bit baggy, but you look brilliant!'

William turned to the long mirror hanging inside the wardrobe, and was faced with his reflection for the very first time. Looking at his grey, scaly skin which poked from the oversized folds of lumpy fabric, he was surprised to see how strange he looked in comparison to Marina. His tentacle hair wobbled like jelly and his face appeared almost hollow next to hers, which was flushed with warmth. The clothes, very clearly meant for a fully-grown man almost twice his size, didn't help much.

'You look like Dad,' Marina beamed. 'I mean, a very pale, teenage Dad. *Very* pale.'

William smiled sweetly at the thought. 'I believe you, by the way,' he said.

'About what?' Marina asked, confused and caught slightly off guard.

'I believe your father is out there. It's only a matter of time before he comes home.'

A lump formed in Marina's throat, which she attempted to swallow with an unsuccessful gulp. 'I'd like to think he will,' she said almost to herself. 'Perhaps he has amnesia, and was rescued in the middle of the night by some wandering sea turtles who took him to France. Once he has his memory back, he'll appear on the horizon in his fishing boat and return to us.'

'If not, we can find him together,' said William as he turned back to the mirror to study his reflection.

Marina clutched his claw as her eyes began to water.

'Really?'

'Definitely,' he beamed.

'MARINA?'

The two friends both jumped at the new voice, which was followed through the house by an explosion of shouts and cheers. Once the front door slammed shut on the noise, Sally Minnow came rushing into the bedroom wearing her greasy white apron and a battered paper hat, loose hair sticking to her face.

'There you both are, thank goodness you're up already.' She scrutinized William with a look of deep confusion. 'What on earth are you wearing?'

'Mum, what are you doing home? What's all that noise?'

'It is amazing, Marina,' said her mother. 'I arrived to open the shop this morning and there were over a dozen fishermen waiting on the wharf, ready to sell to me before anyone else.'

'Oh, wow, that's great! I'm so pleased for you, Mum. What's brought that on?'

The question hung in the air between them for the shortest of moments before they both turned in unison, their eyes falling silently on their house guest. William was still looking in the mirror, now attempting to flatten an especially sticky-uppy tentacle as the realization dawned on Marina. 'They want to see William. Oh no, was that last night's mob outside again?'

'Yes,' admitted Sally. 'I just need to take him to the shop with me. It's not as bad as we thought last night, they're all just excited and curious, really! I think they realize that he's more than just a fish. Also, I've had the most brilliant idea . . . We can sell William's sashimi, and maybe attempt some sushi rolls too! Once people try it, we'll make an absolute fortune, I'm sure of it. Just think how sick everyone is of eating battered cod and chips.'

'But, Mum, I was going to take him snorkelling today! We have to find out what that person has dumped in the sea. If it really is connected to William, they'll be even more desperate to cover their tracks now that he's washed up on the beach.'

'Whatever's down there won't be moving any time soon, Marina. You can snorkel later in the week. William wants to come and help me at the shop! Don't you, William?'

Sally turned back to smile at William as Marina pleaded with him wordlessly, straining so hard that an observer would have thought that her eyeballs might burst from their sockets. Her mother stood, arms folded and blushing pink with excitement.

'Of course,' answered William. 'If I can help you at all, Mrs Minnow, then I'd like to. It's the least I can do.'

'Brilliant!' roared Sally. 'Let's get those clothes off, then. You've made him look truly bizarre, Marina.'

'But, Mum . . .'

'Not another word. It's Saturday. Why don't you go and see what some of your other friends are up to? Snorkelling can wait!'

And with that, Marina was abandoned on the doorstep as Sally swept the boy from the sea off towards the high street with a huge cheer from the enormous crowd of onlookers who trailed behind them. The sun was only now rising above the town as its light reflected off William's newly bare scales, a thousand iridescent colours twinkling goodbye. He turned to wave at Marina, still clutching the travel fan mist-spray she had insisted he take to keep moist as camera bulbs flashed in his face. She knew it was silly to try and explore the sea without him, expert swimmer that he was, but her curiosity was too great. With the excitement of a proper quest at her feet, Marina was finally on the brink of a real-life adventure and once the mystery was solved, William was going to help find her father. Wasting even one second longer in her life of stories was unthinkable.

Dashing back to her room, she pulled a waterproof bag from the wardrobe and started to gather the necessary equipment: her goggles and snorkel, a pair of flippers, a warm towel from the airing cupboard, a thermos full of tea and a box of fish fingers (for much-needed energy).

CHAPTER FIFTEEN

The Search

Marina stood on the beach in her blue swimming costume with the kit bag at her feet, the foamy surf lapping at her bright pink flippers. Edie Krill and Thea Marigold had been waiting, like they'd promised they would, once Marina had explained her plan over the phone. Now they looked on curiously, as their friend attempted to tie an enormous wet rope into a working lasso.

'No, you're doing it *all* wrong!' came a voice from behind them. Peter Featherfin had climbed over one of the long wooden groynes that divided the beach and was shuffling towards the girls, carrying a bucket of sloshy water and a rusty old crabbing line.

'What would you know?' cried Marina, frustrated and wrestling even harder with the stubborn rope that refused to bend to her wishes.

'She's trying to make a lasso,' said Thea. 'It's not going very well.'

Marina swung around to face her young friend with a withering glare that forced the year seven to shrink inside her fluffy hood.

'Well, you need to do a Honda knot, then! Just do a loose overhand knot, then a tight one at the end and feed it back through the loose one before tightening it.'

Marina's mouth fell slack as she listened to the alien words coming from Peter's mouth, with just as little understanding as she had for how he could have room for three bowls of seafood stew every single lunchtime. He might as well have been speaking French for all the sense it made to her.

'You do know what an overhand knot is, Marina?' he asked.

'Of course she doesn't,' interrupted Edie with a smirk. 'When have you ever seen her listen in class? She got detention last week for trying to shave the beard from a mussel with her mum's blunt razor.'

'Well, how do you expect to get a job in the fish industry if you can't even tie an overhand knot?'

'I don't *want* to get a job in the *fish* industry!' cried Marina in a rage.

'But...' Now Peter was the one flummoxed. 'What else is there to do in Merlington?'

'As soon as we've helped William solve this mystery, we're jumping in a boat and setting off to find my dad. He'll be out there somewhere, plucked from the water by an enormous pelican and carried to safety in its beak. He'll be waiting for me to find him.' Marina continued to wring the long snake of rope between her blistering hands in exasperation. 'And I'd be able to do that, if I could just... tie – this – LASSO!'

For fear of Marina giving herself extreme rope burn, or even twisting her hands out of their sockets, Peter crept forward and took the rope himself, dropping his bucket which toppled to the ground, allowing a dozen small crabs to scurry away to freedom in every direction.

'Honestly, Marina,' started Edie. 'All this talk of adventure and going off to find your dad. I'd worry you were serious if I actually thought it was possible.'

'I'm deadly serious, you'll see,' said Marina. 'Once we find out what was dumped in the water on Thursday night, everything will change. William has *already* changed everything – he's proved that nothing is impossible.'

'Here you go!' beamed Peter, who had finished his Honda knot and was proudly presenting a fully formed lasso, which Marina seized in excitement, forgetting the cumbersome flippers she wore and tripping over them to land face first in the sand.

'Well, what now?' asked an increasingly impatient Edie, as Marina pulled herself up from the surf and aggressively rubbed grains of sand from her tongue, spitting and spluttering.

'I'm going to look for what was dumped in the water, of course,' she replied. 'You can hold the end of the rope while I swim out with the lasso round my waist. If I find something, I'll try and tie it round whatever it is and tug the line for you to help pull it to shore.'

'Pull it to shore?' cried Edie, looking aghast from

Marina to the tiny Thea, who was still cowering in her cosy hood like a small turtle. 'This thing was heavy enough to knock William out! How are the two of us supposed to haul it in from the sea with only a rope?'

'I'll push from the other end, in between breaths if it's not too deep. And Peter will help too, of course!'

'I will?' asked Peter, rejoining the conversation, having been happily snuffling a large bag of chocolate-covered clams pulled from the depths of his crabbing kit.

'You'll turn into a clam, Peter Featherfin!' cried Edie, dissolving into giggles at the stern look Marina shot her. The eel pie incident was still a touchy subject . . .

'Oh, don't start that again. What are you even looking for?'

'I'm not quite sure,' said Marina, stepping into the lasso, which she tightened at her waist. She pointed at a flashing red buoy floating in the distance. 'William was somewhere near that light when he was knocked unconscious, and we're standing in the very spot he washed up yesterday afternoon. If I swim out in a straight line towards the buoy, I'm bound to find something. I'll know it when I see it!'

'How many near-drowning experiences do you need in one week?' Edie called, shaking her head in disbelief.

Marina let the comment slide, as she snapped on her goggles and took her first tentative steps into the nippy autumn sea, which was even colder than she'd anticipated. The chill crept up her legs with an unpleasant prickle before a wave broke across her stomach, showering her in water. She hoped her shocked yelp hadn't carried back to the beach and her friends, and to save face immediately popped the snorkel in her mouth and dived into the next oncoming wave.

Under the surface, the cold whipped Marina's skin as she swam quickly to fight off the sting. Her flippers propelled her along and as she gathered her thoughts, she realized how hard it was to see through the misty water of the Channel. What a silly idea it had been not to wait for William. Sure, she was able to make out the seabed clearly for now, but by the time she was deep enough to find whatever this important piece of evidence was, it would almost be impossible to see through the gloom.

She swam onwards anyway, continuing straight

from the point William had washed up on the shore – her face pointing downwards and probing the seabed like a helicopter searchlight. As the sand sloped deeper and deeper, Marina knew it wouldn't be long before she'd lose visibility entirely and would have no hope of seeing where to tie her lasso. She watched a blurry lobster scurry along the sand with a small fish between its claws, appreciated the calming effect a garden of swaying seaweed had on her nerves, and let out a laugh of bubbles when she spotted a busted toilet seat through the murky green haze.

Then something much more exciting caught her eye. Out of place, nestled in the sand but standing out like a sore thumb, having barely had time to get tangled in the weeds of the bay. She knew instantly it was what she had been searching for. A trunk, or chest, padlocked and calling out to Marina with a teasing promise: *I have secrets for you.*

As she leant her face in further, caught as if the chest had a tidal pull of its own, Marina's snorkel dipped beneath the surface and immediately filled her mouth with disgusting, salty water.

Back on the shore, Edie, Thea and Peter watched with concern.

'It looks like she's drowning,' said Thea matter-of-factly, pulling back her hood to get a better view. 'Do you think we should call someone?'

'She's just inhaling seawater,' scowled Edie, sticking out her tongue and gagging at the thought.

'No, she's definitely drowning. She's waving her arms in the air and shouting! Oh no, we've killed her!'

Edie held a hand to her forehead, shielding her eyes from the sun. 'Don't be stupid, she's smiling now. Look!'

'Edie's right,' said Peter. 'She must have found something!'

CHAPTER SIXTEEN

A Padlock in Place

*F*orty minutes later, each of them panting with exhaustion having pulled and pushed the heavy object into the shallows, Marina had rejoined her friends on the beach and they stared down at their soaking wet bounty.

An elegant antique trunk, with solid wood feet and polished brass corners, stood on the sand before them. It was clearly weathered by age but hardly at all by the sea, so it couldn't have spent very long submerged. A dark red leather ran along the mouth of its opening like a thin, villainous lip, desperate to peel open and scream its secrets. Now a large brass padlock was the only thing in the way. Surely it would be too great a coincidence for the items hidden inside, abandoned so recklessly in the night, not to offer some answers about William?

'Well, that was fun . . .' said Edie sarcastically, still catching her breath.

'The padlock looks pretty thick. I don't suppose this mysterious midnight sailor lobbed the key overboard as well?' Peter said, laughing, before restraining himself at the sight of Marina's unimpressed glare.

She was shivering from the cold of the sea and wrapped herself tightly in the fluffy blue towel from her kit bag. She knelt to find her thermos, before burning her tongue on the still-scalding tea and proceeding to slurp it in smaller, safer mouthfuls.

'How are we going to get it open?' she asked, frustration fizzing through her. 'It would take ages to drag it all the way home, even if we *did* then manage to prise it off with some pliers.'

'We could smash it open with a rock!' cried Thea suddenly.

'It's a padlock, not a coconut,' muttered Edie, her eyes rolling so hard they almost disappeared into the back of her head.

'Does anyone have a better idea?' questioned Thea.

She was met with silence as Edie, Marina and Peter looked at one another in doubt. Lacking any suggestions of their own, each of them sank to the ground and began to scour the sand for a decent tool. Marina scooped up a large shard of flint and began to stab at the dirty padlock, taking turns with Edie who was trying to bash in the chest itself with a small but hard granite pebble. Peter, having mistaken a dozing crab fresh from his own bucket for a stone, was now desperately trying to fight off the crustacean as it swung from the tip of his finger.

'Look out! Coming through!'

Marina turned from her ineffective jabbing just in time to dive out of the way as Thea, carrying an enormous rock over her head, threw it down and smashed the padlock from its place in one try.

'Flipping hake, Thea!' cried Edie, picking herself up from the huge pile of sand she'd leapt into as the boulder came hurtling past. 'You almost took my head off!'

'Well, it didn't look as though your pebble was quite up to the job.'

'I was getting somewhere; I could feel it. If you'd given me a little warning...'

'Look!' yelled Thea, shushing Edie into silence.

Marina was running her fingers along the damp leather lining at the mouth of the chest.

'Do it,' encouraged Edie.

Peter stumbled to his knees by the group, having finally flung the crab from his fingertip. 'Open it, then,' he puffed.

'Go on!' beamed Thea.

Struck by a moment of uncertainty, and almost choking on adrenaline, Marina hesitated for a few seconds, before slipping her fingers under the lid and throwing it open. She did it with such force that the very screws holding the thing in place crumbled to dust, the lid snapping free and skidding down the sand dunes to the water behind.

'Well, why didn't we just try that in the first place?' scowled Edie.

'It must be super old. What's inside?' shrieked Thea from behind her hands, hiding her face from sheer excitement.

A soggy stench of salt burst through Marina's nostrils as she leant over the trunk, reaching her hands inside and grasping the first item that met her eyes. A soft, cuddly sea turtle, with black button eyes and a green ribbon tied neatly at its neck. Almost pristine, it was a toy that had never been loved, and certainly never been played with. If it hadn't been soaking wet, Marina would have sworn that it was brand new.

'It doesn't make any sense,' said Peter, who stood at her shoulder. He sank his arms deep inside the trunk and rifled through the contents, pulling out several babygrows. Each one seemed to have had the cotton sleeves clumsily cut away, and they were all patterned with sailing boats, blue stars or an array of multi-coloured fish. 'Why would someone have bothered to chuck all of this stuff in the sea?'

'Maybe they didn't want anyone to know they had it,' suggested Thea.

'Maybe someone was trying to keep the fact they'd had a baby a secret,' Peter mused.

The suggestion forced a memory to the forefront of Marina's mind, and not for the first time that morning. The memory of Granny Minnow's story – of cockles and nets and tentacle hair.

'But what can any of this have to do with William?' asked Edie, dropping to her knees and pulling a pile of dripping wet nursery books from the trunk. She began to peel back the pages, which clung together like a sticky plaster on a hairy knee. 'It's so totally random. Marina, what do you think?'

Marina had taken a step back from the group. She stood near the edge of the promenade in the shadow of the rising cliffs, looking at her friends who still huddled around the mysterious trunk, and clutching the stuffed turtle tightly to her chest. She squeezed it, unintentionally wringing from it a stream of salty water that trickled down her legs to land on her wriggling toes in the sand.

'I think I need to visit my granny.'

CHAPTER SEVENTEEN

Booming

*T*he notion of a town with seventeen fishmongers would make the hardiest of fishy businessmen think twice before setting up shop, let alone in a place as small as Merlington. With the bulk of its fisheries based on the high street, the rest trickling around the corner of the seafront and up into the cliffs, the competition could be viewed as unassailable. But every shop had its purpose. Sole Brothers, run by

Alan and Ian Thropp at the edge of the beach, sold delicious trays of fried scallops and oysters at lunchtime. Shrimpy's could be relied on for meaty fillets of the most tender salmon and tuna, while Clam Baked and its owner Cheryl Shoal took pride in their generous helpings of crab broth and lobster bisque. And then, of course, there was Harold Mole's fleet of stores headed up by Mullet Over, the jewel in his crown, famed for its premium shellfish and beautifully presented Catch of the Day.

While the many fishmongers of Merlington enjoyed relative success with the town's seafood-hungry residents, Minnow's was the exception, often lucky just to make ends meet, thanks to Harold's intimidation tactics and his widely accepted boycott of the business. That was, until a certain tentacle-haired young man washed ashore.

Minnow's was booming. Not just with fish – the most dazzling display of prawns, skate, lobster, mussels, tuna, sea bass and all other types of enticing and delicious produce filled the display cabinets to suffocation – Sally Minnow's modest store was also booming with customers. A thick queue spilt from the narrow front door and down the high street, past a local television van just pulling up to the scene. The Mullet Over itself would be hard pushed to do such good trade, even at the height of summer.

Wendy Whitby wriggled her way into the crowd, ducking and diving through the mass of people, then sneaking between Mrs Cuttle's wide legs before they snapped shut behind her. Reaching the front of the shop, she peered up at the counter, staring at the faces of what seemed like two dozen king crabs, who all returned her gaze – their eyes pressed against the cold glass slowly turning white with condensation, as if from their fevered breath.

'I was here first,' cried Mrs Cuttle, glaring at Wendy down her round, upturned nose. 'Don't think you'll get to see him before I do, girl. I'm not above pushing!'

Wendy took a step back, landing on the toes of her best friend, Daisy Baitman.

'Did you see him yet, Wendy? His claws are as sharp as a fishmonger's knife! I can't wait to try his sashimi, it sounds so fancy,' she said, glowing.

'Don't tell me you've been brainwashed by all of this too,' Wendy spat. 'The whole thing is an absolute joke. I'm convinced more than ever that it's some stupid prank Marina's dreamt up just to get back at me.'

'You were there on the beach,' countered Daisy. 'You saw him along with the rest of us! He's got *claws* for hands, Wendy. Pincers!'

'They're probably giant foam gloves,' Wendy muttered, not quite believing it herself. She knew Marina would be lapping up this attention, and it was *already* too irritating to bear. From what she'd over-heard from her father, who brought home all the best gossip thanks to being landlord of The Laughing Trout, Marina's family had been on the brink of bankruptcy, but all of this publicity might actually do them good. Wendy wasn't a spiteful girl (at least *she* didn't think she was), but she was furious to see the extent of the Minnows' newfound celebrity.

'Oh my *cod*, Wendy, look!' Daisy screamed in delight.

The great shape of Mrs Cuttle had begun to sidestep through the crowd with a brown bag that overflowed with seafood, and the entire shop counter became fully visible for the first time. At one end, Marina's spindly mother stood behind an ancient till, stuffing tens and twenties into the overflowing cash drawer. Wendy wanted to scream when she saw the grin stretched across her face, which was a mirror of Marina at her most unbearable. Daisy grabbed her friend's chin and gently pushed it round to face the other end of the counter, and Wendy's eyes fell on William. His scales glistened from the light of the reflective metal worktop, as his absurd tentacle hair swayed and pulsated at his shoulders. The girls stood, openly gawping, before the impossible boy threw an entire sea bass over his head and cut a claw through the air. Seconds later, the perfectly descaled fish fell gently on to the counter and the room erupted in applause.

'Incredible!' cheered Daisy, throwing her fist in the air before smacking her hands together in excitement. Wendy clipped her round the head.

'Oh, don't you start!'

Mrs Cuttle crashed back through the front door, panting as she knocked several customers to the floor with her widely splayed elbows, flinging grey prawns through the air.

'What did I miss?' she cried. 'Did he chop something?'

Suddenly Sally Minnow was at Wendy and Daisy's

shoulders, still beaming from ear to ear and carrying a tray of what looked like raw fish.

'Would you young ladies care to try some of William's delicious sashimi?'

William. They're still acting like this freak is a regular kid, thought Wendy.

'Oh, yes please, Mrs Minnow,' cooed Daisy without hesitation, missing the death stare her fuming friend shot at her back.

'And how about you . . . You're Walter's daughter, aren't you? Wendy, isn't it?' asked Sally kindly, lowering the sashimi in offering.

'I'm OK, thank you.'

'Oh, go on, you'll love it! I know it sounds like an odd thing to want to eat, but William really is an expert when it comes to the delicacies of seafood.'

'I'll take your word for it,' dismissed Wendy.

'I insist!'

Marina's mother held the tray directly in front of her young customer's face. If only to get rid of her, Wendy finally gave in and picked up a thin piece of salmon sashimi between her thumb and forefinger with as much caution as if it were a hand grenade.

'Enjoy!' cheered Sally, moving on into the crowd,

which seemed to grow thicker and more fevered with every second.

'Are you going to try it?' encouraged Daisy, popping a portion of tuna between her lips and giving a squeak of delight.

'Am I hake!' Wendy roared, shoving the salmon into her coat pocket and darting back towards the door. She had to swerve out of the way as a cameraman charged inside, followed closely by a man she knew was a reporter for the local news.

Brilliant, now Marina's head will be bigger than ever, thought Wendy. *It's as if she's the only girl in the whole of Merlington who matters.*

CHAPTER EIGHTEEN

Carpe Diem

*W*alter Whitby stood across the road as he watched his daughter burst furiously through the horde of bodies huddled outside Minnow's. He grumbled to himself, spitting out a blob of chewed tobacco, which bubbled on the pavement like tar. Enticed by the action and the fish oil-soaked scalp of Walter's companion, a hungry seagull dived towards them. Harold Mole calmly ducked low enough for the bird to miss its target and crash instead into the side of Walter's face.

'This won't do,' tutted Harold, as his bony friend fought off the battered gull now clawing at his cheek. 'No, this won't do at all.'

'I told you,' cried Walter, smacking the gull into the sky with a scrawny fist before it hovered away in confusion. 'Look at these mindless suckers, all 'ere because they want t'see some kid with claws. The rest of the town is totally dead, an' I mean dead. Even my pub!'

Harold scratched his chin as he took another huge bite of crabmeat from his overstuffed fist. 'This definitely will not do.'

Wendy wrapped her arms around her father's waist as she reached the miserable pair, joining them in staring daggers at the queue spilling out of Minnow's, which was blocking the empty doorways of several other deserted fishmongers.

'Tell us, Wendy,' invited Harold.

'I could barely breathe in there, it's so full of gawping losers. Mrs Cuttle almost squashed me between her legs I was so—'

'What about the creature?'

'You mean *William*?' laughed Wendy irritably. 'That's what they call him, like he's some kid who's come to Merlington for a holiday.'

'William,' said Harold. The name felt strange on his tongue and a peculiar feeling ran through him at the knowledge of it. 'And did you get a glimpse of this Japanese-style sashimi everyone's been banging on about?'

'She practically forced it down my throat,' said Wendy, reaching into her pocket and pulling out the battered piece of perfectly sliced salmon. The fish was sweating in the daylight, its orange flesh damp with oil. Without missing a beat, Harold snatched it greedily from Wendy's palm and threw it into his wide-open mouth.

'*Humph*,' groaned Harold, chewing angrily as his face began to turn a deep shade of beetroot. 'It's delicious.'

Clenching his fists, he squeezed his remaining crabsticks so tightly that processed meat spewed from between his hairy knuckles and dripped into a sickly heap on the ground. A nearby squabble of seagulls, waiting on a rooftop for their moment to swoop on Harold's putrid scalp, were very happy instead to feast on this more substantial meal.

'We've got to do something about it – and soon.'

'Harold, just leave it, mate,' Walter moaned. 'Sally's never gonna sell the place – you need t'move on with your life.'

'You think this is still just about me getting that extension built?' asked Harold in bewilderment. 'This is about so much more than a state-of-the-art industrial walk-in freezer, believe me!'

Walter coughed in surprise. Harold had spent countless evenings hunched over the bar in The Laughing Trout, lecturing him on the benefits of chrome versus aluminium insulation.

'This is about Merlington!' Harold cried. 'When I swore my oath as Prime Warden of the Reverential Federation of Fishmongers, I promised to uphold the honour of this noble fishing town. The name Merlington might not mean much to some people, but if we let these rabble-rousers turn our home into a circus sideshow act there'll be no going back.'

Wendy, having grown bored of the adults' conversation, had returned across the street to press her nose against the front window of Minnow's. Staring through the glass she caught the eye of Sally Minnow, who smiled at her with genuine warmth. Wendy felt a ripple of guilt in her stomach, which she pushed down to her toes with another vision of Marina's smug, smarmy face.

'Did you know Jasper Jenkins went to Minnow's first this morning, even before the Mullet Over?' Harold spat. 'He sold the best of his fish to *her* before he even thought about coming to my flagship store. I had to watch as fisherman after fisherman plied her with produce all morning! The managers of my other five stores barely had anything left to choose from once I'd filled my freezer.'

'Is that why Carp-e Diem is closed?' mused Walter.

'Don't be ridiculous. Why would Carp-e Diem be closed?' barked Harold.

'Because Caroline Carp is over there, inside Minnow's.'

The blood drained from Harold's face. Through the window, he watched Caroline Carp flap with genuine delight at William's expert claw work. She clapped her hands in glee, her eyes watering happily as she bought a large brown bag brimful of sashimi.

The manager of Harold's third-largest shop, Caroline was a tall woman with a delicate face framed by a curly blonde bob. After taking on the job as manager of Carp-e Diem, she had enjoyed a long and loving relationship with Harold, so much so that he had even renamed the shop for her. But since their sudden break-up the years had soured their bond, and to this day Caroline remained one of the few people on the payroll that Harold had little control over.

Catching his eye now as she dabbed her own with a handkerchief, Caroline made her way through the crowds and out on to the high street, and her fleeting smile of relief hardened into a frown that was filled with resentment. She crossed the road to meet her bitter boss.

'Afternoon, Harold.'

'Caroline,' he seethed. 'What exactly do you think you are doing? You know better than to be associating with Minnow and that...' He spluttered, refusing to name the strange boy. '*That!*'

'I was under the impression that I was a grown woman and free to do as I please.'

'You are the proprietor of a Harold Mole establishment and you are tarnishing my good name by hanging around with these miscreants and their freaky friends. I will not have it.'

Harold gave Caroline a hard stare, which she

returned, unblinking, with an effortlessly unfazed eyebrow raise.

'I shall continue to visit whichever stores I like, and will associate with whomever I see fit. I've learnt my lesson in *that* regard.'

She turned on her heel, leaving in her wake a trail of unusual perfume which found its way directly into Harold's furiously flared nostrils.

'We shall talk about this again, Caroline!' he yelled after her.

'D'you let all your old girlfriends talk to you like that, Harold?' Walter chuckled, popping a fresh piece of tobacco between his teeth. 'You're losin' your touch, pal.'

'She's not worth the bother,' Harold whispered, still watching Caroline as she retreated down the high street towards the Carp-e Diem, his eyes moving in time to the bounce of her curls.

'What do you s'pose we do, then, Harold?' asked Walter, scratching his head with pained perplexity. 'It looks like this fish lad might be 'ere t'stay.'

'Leave it to me,' Harold replied ominously. He turned back to face Minnow's, his resentful eyes on William, who was sharpening his claws for a cameraman to the cheers of the crowd still bulging from the shop door. A plan was beginning to take shape, and if Walter hadn't known better, he could have sworn he saw the shadow of a smile forming in the creases of the fishmonger's face.

CHAPTER NINETEEN

Mothballs and Mint

$\mathcal{T}$he Minnow matriarch lived in a care home for the elderly at the top of a craggy bluff east of the harbour, high above the sleepy town of Merlington. Following her son's disappearance and presumed death, Geraldine Minnow's memory had deteriorated rapidly. It had started with little things – misplacing her car keys in the freezer or frying up sliced apple instead of potato with her battered cod – but had quickly progressed to forgetting where she lived and even her own granddaughter's face in just a few months. It was with a heavy heart that Sally Minnow had been forced to place her mother-in-law in a home, a decision she felt guilt over daily. But there was nothing else that could have been done. Marina had only been very small at the time, and with a fledgling business to save, there was no other way Sally would have coped.

The afternoon sun hung low in the sky by the time Marina approached the grand, gothic-looking building. She was full of questions she knew her grandmother likely wouldn't be able to answer, but she needed to try all the same. It was with apprehension that she looked up at the imposing structure, precariously perched on the cliff-side. Black iron railings lined the teal-coloured roof of slanted wood, which slipped down into grey stone columns sprinkled with panes of grubby glass. Far below, the breaking waves threatened to eat away at the earth and bring the entire home crashing into the sea.

Entering the building, Marina was hit by a familiar scent that only tightened the knot of guilt in her stomach. A musty clash of mothballs and mint, which fought against the warm smell of a recently hoovered carpet. She hadn't visited in several weeks, but since it had become painfully obvious that Granny Minnow didn't notice either way, that just felt . . . easier.

Marina walked up to the dusty reception desk. It was occupied by the manager's teenage daughter, who filed her nails and cawed like a crow as her phone dinged with text message alerts. After she dotted the last 'i' of her surname in the guestbook, Marina's attention was drawn by a small television in the cosy lounge behind that hummed happily to several residents sitting in thick, lacy armchairs. The southern tones of 'Big Mouth' Billy were pouring from the tinny speakers and the screen filled with the smiling face of her mother, clutching William under one arm and standing behind the counter at Minnow's. As Sally looked directly into the camera, wearing an enormous grin, Marina was certain that she'd be able to count every one of her mother's teeth.

'. . . and the most amazing part is, it's totally raw! Totally raw and *totally* delicious. I promise you, Sally's Salivating Sashimi (trademark pending) is the tastiest thing to hit the southern coast since the invention of fish batter!'

'Now tell us more about how you discovered William,' said the reporter off-screen. 'He really is quite the exceptional young man.'

'That he is,' beamed Sally, pulling her new apprentice closer as his tentacles waved wildly at her side. 'It's as if William has been sent to us as a gift. We've been living under a cloud of uncertainty for so long here at Minnow's, he's like a guardian angel come to help save the day. By slicing everyone delicious sashimi!'

Marina couldn't believe what she was seeing . . .

'Isn't it crazy?' interrupted the young receptionist, pulling Marina from her trance. 'My friends have been down at that place all morning. Look at this!'

She scrolled through some messages on her phone before pushing the device into Marina's face. There in a photo on-screen stood a perplexed-looking William with three spotty teenage girls – two held up strands of his tentacle hair like rubbery antlers, while the other clutched his claw in her fist as though it were a trophy.

'Wild, right?' gushed the receptionist, whom Marina looked at with a mixture of bemusement and concern. 'I wonder if he's got a girlfriend.'

'I . . . I've no idea,' she mumbled, still in shock as the girl looked up from the phone to face her with a glare.

'Either way, I'm heading there as soon as visiting hours are finally done!' she declared, urging Marina up the stairs with her eyes.

Tearing herself from the television, Marina moved away from the front desk and began her ascent of the narrow, chintz-lined staircase which led her up the four flights to the attic bedroom that housed her grandmother. Taking a deep breath, she knocked on the door three times.

'Granny?' she called, opening the door without waiting for an answer and peering into the bright but small room.

Granny Minnow sat in a red velvet armchair perched beneath the open window, baking herself in the autumn sunshine which poured through a net curtain gently flapping in the breeze. Marina was comforted to see her leathery skin as brown as ever, and the familiar wisp of white hair still curled into a pristine cloud on top of her head. As usual, Granny's eyelashes were so thickly caked in mascara that she was forced to throw her head backwards at a ninety-degree angle to see. She did so now, and her eyelids flapped open like some kind of backwards china doll before her pupils perused her granddaughter's apprehensive face.

'I don't know *what* you're selling, but I'm not interested. I've got enough cleaning brushes, thank you very much!'

'Granny, it's me. Marina.'

The woman looked hard through her blackened eyelashes and down her nose at the girl whose face she'd long since forgotten.

'Ah, my mistake. Chocolate chip cookies, is it? Girl Guides? I just bought some shortbread the other day from that odd one with the glasses. I've never had much of a sweet tooth, really.' That was a lie. Geraldine's fondness for a chocolate fondant had been the cause of some quite severe tooth decay and the loss of all but three teeth. She had been forced to wear a comically large set of dentures since the age of fifty-five.

'I'm not selling anything, Granny. I just wanted to come and see how you were.' Marina felt awful as the white lie touched her lips, knowing it was a thirst for information that had really brought her up the cliff path. 'How are you doing? Are they looking after you properly?'

'Listen here, girl. I'm no invalid! I could still dance the tango 'til dawn if I wanted to.'

Marina knew she was getting nowhere and the pleasantries were all but pointless.

'Granny, I need your help. I know it's hard for you to remember stuff, but I need you to think about something really specific. A story you told me, a long time ago, about a fisherman's catch. Do you remember how we used to like telling each other stories?'

Marina's grandmother continued to survey the young girl's face with curiosity and suspicion. She listened, trying to make sense of both the words and the small person whose mouth they came from, now nestled in the wing-backed leather armchair opposite.

'Do you remember the fisherman, Granny? The one in that tale about the really peculiar catch?' Marina pleaded, frustration and sadness bubbling behind her eyes like sea foam.

'Fisherman? My son is a fisherman.'

Marina felt a tickle in her heart at the mention of her father. It had been a long time since anyone had spoken of him in the present tense. It was one of the main reasons that these visits were so difficult to manage.

'He's such a handsome boy, my son. Now, don't you be bothering him with your cookies either! His waistline has seen better days, that's for sure.'

Marina had known this would be hard, but she'd forgotten how seeing her grandmother so disconnected from reality was almost too painful to bear.

'No, Granny. I mean a different fisherman. This fisherman caught something very special. Something he kept at the old pier in secret . . .'

Granny's eyes narrowed with a sharp burst of understanding. 'What are you blithering on about, Marina? Of course I remember him, dear,' she said. 'It's not like I'd forget that in a hurry now, is it?'

'What, Granny, what was the story?'

Marina held back the urge to leap on her grandmother's knee and wring the information from her, giddy with the excitement at the prospect of solving the riddle that had played on her mind for days. Granny had been overcome by a powerful wave of clarity and not a moment more could be wasted.

CHAPTER TWENTY

Granny's Story

'I remember,' continued Geraldine, shifting in her seat as the familiar show of pomp and pageantry took over. 'He was out at sea very late one evening, when the weather was especially bizarre – the kind of night where the promise of a storm holds electricity in the air. When the world seems somehow sharper, and the atoms in the sky are visible to the naked eye, buzzing and floating about your head.'

Marina listened in wonder. Her grandmother's voice was strong and clear, her eyes engaged and filled with warmth, as the story poured from her like water. It felt cosy and familiar, and was enough to make tears of comfort well in the corners of Marina's own eyes.

'This particular fisherman had never had much luck, to be perfectly honest. He would watch the other men hauling in their great nets of haddock, cod, trout – every type of fish and seafood you'd hope to come across on the south coast. And this night had been no different. He lay there in his boat, the only man left at sea in the pouring rain, continuing to scour the waves for a catch, having only pulled up a few prawns and an old copper kettle all day. *At least I can sell that on as scrap metal*, he thought.

'And then he saw it – the faintest shape of another rowing boat on the water, before the silhouette of a person took form through the haze of the storm. Rain lashed at the figure's back as a tight bundle left their arms and flew into the sky, landing in the violent waves with a splash. Then the stranger fled quickly into the night. The fisherman's curiosity was stirred. He rowed slowly towards the same spot and threw his empty net into the water, waiting.

'After a few minutes, feeling a sharp tug at the end of his net, he leapt to the edge of the boat in excitement. He looked down into the dark waves and heaved. It turned out to be a surprisingly light load as he leant backwards, and before long he fell to the floor with a final wrench as the contents of the net spilt at his feet. Some more lousy shells and cockles, an old leather boot . . . And a slimy, grey squid. Nothing that was worth coming all the way out here to dump in the middle of a storm, but something tasty for tomorrow's dinner at least! But no, there was something not quite right about the way the squid flopped about on the deck. It had a body, and beneath the tentacles, a face. Arms, legs, a rubbery torso covered in iridescent scales, but a creature with a human face. A baby.'

Marina, hooked on every word, began to cough, choking in surprise as she realized she hadn't inhaled a breath for several moments. *She'd been right*. This was William. Granny Minnow's story was about William!

'It was a baby with human features, but clearly a child of the ocean; a son of Poseidon who now returned the fisherman's gaze with a matched curiosity. Someone had clearly been keen to keep this peculiar baby a secret, rowing out into the darkness to dispose of it. So what was the fisherman supposed to do now? He could hardly take the creature home, not knowing who could have gone to such great lengths to be rid of the wretched thing. But he couldn't bring himself to toss an innocent baby back into the ocean, whether it belonged there or not. He was struck by a thought, in that moment, that he had been witness to this act of unkindness for a reason. He was meant to have been here, all along, so that the child could find its way into his empty fishing net. He had been chosen to care for the boy, by the very water itself.

'Looking back to shore and to the seafood-obsessed town of Merlington, most of its residents fast asleep in their beds, the fisherman's eyes strained to see through the downpour. Finally he spied the bait shop, perched on the last remaining legs of the old wooden pier which had burnt from the inside out in a fire a few years prior, its walkway collapsed into the sea and now completely cut off from land. It seemed like the only option – an insane plan, perfect for an insane turn of events. Inside the bait shop the baby would have warmth, and damp, and plenty of food at its pincer-tips. They could hide there quite happily, while the fisherman found out more – what he was, where he came from, and whether he might still be in danger.

'He visited early each morning, feeding the child what he could spare from his own meagre catches. He would bathe him in saltwater, removing the barnacles from the child's skin that seemed to grow like hair. As the months went by and the mystery of the stranger remained unsolved, he sought to make a home for the boy – carrying over blankets and toys, and teaching him to read from tin cans and old bottles, anything that could survive in the damp of a home in the open ocean. And soon, protecting him became more than a job. He saw him with a father's eyes, and the love that grew in his heart fought daily with the fear deep in his stomach at the thought of what this desperate person would do if they were to ever know the child's existence had been discovered.

'With the shack truly abandoned, and the wooden walkway from the beach turning to dust at the bottom of the sea, the fisherman was happy to encourage the other sailors to stay well away. They began to share the other-worldly stories that he planted in their minds, overheard in late-night conversations at the pub. Tales of disturbing sounds and ghostly goings-on, which soon they all swore they could feel emanating from behind the shadowy walls.

'And so, he kept the child there in the burnt-out old pier as it persisted to crumble. He continued his daily visits by boat in a journey which no one else would dare to make, ensuring that the boy remained his secret, and his burden. But really, that was how the fisherman liked it, and how it had to be.'

Granny Minnow smacked her dry lips in satisfaction as she ended her story, folding her hands in her lap. Leaning back in her chair, she looked up at the window and out to sea as a gull's cry echoed across the cliffs. Marina was caught somewhere between shock and delight as she took in the story for the second time in her life. It felt both familiar, and yet totally astonishing. Images of her new fishy friend danced through her mind. There was no doubt this fisherman was the father William had waited for so patiently all these years. But who could have been so cruel as to throw a baby into the sea? And what had happened next? Why had the fisherman left the old pier one day, never to return?

'Granny,' Marina asked, breaking the silence. 'How do you know this tale?'

The ageing storyteller looked down from the window, her crystal-blue eyes meeting Marina's with intent. 'Why, dear, your father told me, of course.'

Marina stopped dead. Had she heard that correctly? If her father had been the one to pass this story down, did that mean . . .

It couldn't be.

Was it possible that Nigel Minnow *was* the fisherman from his story? If he were, then that meant the adopted father that William yearned for was her very own long-lost dad.

Marina went to sit down, dizziness overcoming her, before realizing she was already perched on the edge of her springy leather armchair.

'*Dad* was the fisherman,' she continued the story aloud. '*He* looked after William for all those years, worried there was someone in town that might still want to hurt him . . . And then, he was gone, and William was left to wait alone. That is, until I found him on the very same night that a trunk filled with baby clothes was thrown into the harbour . . . It has to be connected. Whoever abandoned William at sea might *still* be covering their tracks.'

Thoughts and questions flooded Marina's mind like a succession of waves, new ones breaking every second. But Granny Minnow had already turned back to the window, her eyes clouded over as her brief moment of clarity was washed away, along with her granddaughter's hope of answers.

CHAPTER TWENTY-ONE

Halibut

The rest of the weekend sped by in a blur of interviews, autographs and public appearances for William, while the till at Minnow's continued to be stuffed full of cash. Marina was sure the machine would have been sick from the strange sensation of fullness if it were able.

An entire range of tentacle boy merchandise quickly lined a set of makeshift shelves that ran the length of the store. They overflowed with tea towels, T-shirts and soon an enormous pile of cuddly toys after Sally Minnow put the knitting circle at her mother-in-law's home to work, making the most of their local fame. Sashimi was being sold up and down the high street, the desperate fishmongers of Merlington attempting to replicate the success of Minnow's popular new offering. Unfortunately for them, it was the boy with the crab claws whom people were coming to see in their droves, and who was the reason Minnow's now held the monopoly on local fish overnight.

Marina was no closer to uncovering the truth of William's origins, even after Granny's explosive story. She felt awful, knowing that her father's disappearance was to cause even more heartache once William learnt the truth – that the man he searched for had been missing for the last six years. Having no good news to soften the blow, she had decided it was best to keep these alarming discoveries to herself. This proved to be harder than she had expected.

On Sunday evening, when her mum pulled a leather-bound photo album from a shelf in the living room, Marina shrieked with such horror that Sally forgot all about showing William family pictures.

Marina had to run them through a list of made-up symptoms and was sent to bed immediately – the photo album stuffed up the back of her jumper. There was no way she could allow William to see a more recent photo of her father than those of his wedding, as he would surely be recognizable as the fisherman. Marina slept with the album tucked under her pillow that night, then carrying it in her school bag wherever she went. The antique trunk was safely locked inside Edie's family beach hut, and with no idea as to who had dumped it in the harbour there was no sense in upsetting William just yet with the news that his cherished father was her very own, lost on the sea . . .

'Marina, are you feeling OK?' Edie whispered across the classroom table the next day at school. 'You've been prodding that thing for ages.'

They had been tasked with dissecting an enormous halibut, whose long oval fins spilt across either side of the narrow desk. Marina jabbed its brown flesh with a knife, once again unable to take in the details of the lesson as her mind fizzed anxiously with images of cuddly sea turtles and her father's abandoned fishing net.

'I'm fine,' she lied unconvincingly. 'I've just never been that big a fan of halibut.'

'Well breathe through your mouth. You can't be poorly or you'll miss out on trick-or-treating tonight,' said Edie. It was Halloween, and the whole school was buzzing with excitement.

'Class,' called Mrs Orr. 'Who can tell me what Charles Darwin meant when he discussed the "remarkable peculiarity" that many of these flatfish have in common?'

Wendy Whitby's hand shot into the air, almost knocking her own half-dissected flatfish from the desk and causing her work partner Daisy to frown in disapproval.

'Flatfish are symmetrical at birth like all other fish, with one eye on each side of their head,' she practically screamed. 'But in many species of flatfish, towards the end of their development one eye will migrate to the other side of their skull where it is permanently fixed.'

Marina's insides squirmed at the unpleasant thought. Her face drained of colour to match the pale shade of the halibut's belly. She took several deep breaths to steady her stomach, her mind still racing dizzily.

'Very good, Wendy!' cheered Mrs Orr, walking between the tables to examine the work of her pupils, pausing only to reapply a thick smudge of toothpaste below her nostrils. The stench of fish was beginning to overwhelm the classroom, as the ancient radiators wafted their dusty heat across the desks. Marina continued breathing deeply through her mouth as she watched Edie run a knife down the halibut's backbone. The smell, which had enveloped the room, was transporting her back to the ancient pier. Her head began to spin as an image of her father depositing a tentacled baby behind the shack's damp walls flashed before her eyes.

'Lovely work, Edie,' gagged Mrs Orr as she inhaled minty waves of halibut. She turned to Marina, whose knife wobbled limply in her fist. 'Are you all right, Marina? You're looking a little peaky.'

'I'm fine, I—'

A faint knock on the classroom door suddenly drew their attention. The students dropped their sharp utensils and turned to see a mess of tentacles bobbing in the small window.

'William!' beamed Mrs Orr, her arms in the air as she charged across the room and pulled the door open.

'Sorry,' squirmed William. 'I was here on time but couldn't get the handle to work.' He held up two shiny claws in evidence before waving one enthusiastically at Marina with a smile. She sank back into her chair. It felt as if her two worlds were colliding, as if her restless thoughts had physically summoned William to the classroom.

'Not at all, you're right on time!' Mrs Orr ushered the boy over to the whiteboard. 'Class, William here is kindly joining us for a lesson on slicing sashimi. Won't that be fun?'

The room erupted in cheers, as Marina looked around at her friends' faces to see her own glum expression reflected only in the irritated pout of Wendy Whitby.

A short while later William stood confidently before the class, a fat slab of red tuna draped across his arms like a scarf. Giving Marina a friendly wink, he threw the fish above his head before swishing a claw through the air with almost invisible speed. A heap of blushed sashimi landed on Mrs Orr's desk with a delicate pad, as the goggle-eyed students visibly gawped with open mouths.

'Why the hell do we have to learn this rubbish?' cursed Wendy under her breath. 'This obsession with raw fish can't possibly last much longer.'

'But it's so beautiful,' cheered Daisy, receiving a death stare in return, before addressing William directly, her cheeks turning rosy as his tentacles swayed in her eyeline. 'William, how did you find out that seaweed and raw fish went so well together?'

'An old tin of cat food washed up beside my window.' He smiled wistfully at the memory of the label's listed ingredients. 'Tuna, seaweed, fish broth. I thought it sounded super tasty!'

Daisy's tongue lurched from the side of her mouth in disgust, as she silently wished she had never asked the question.

'William, perhaps you can show the class the best way to hold a knife for slicing sashimi?' directed Mrs Orr, passing around thick slabs of salmon and tuna to each desk.

'I've no idea, to be honest,' he replied. 'I've never had to use a knife.'

Wendy rolled her eyes as Peter Featherfin, sitting directly in front of Mrs Orr's desk, sneaked fistfuls of fish beneath his notebook, shovelling tuna into his mouth whenever the teacher's back was turned.

Armed each with their own fresh fillet of fish, the class began to hack away inelegantly as William sneaked to the back of the room and sat by Marina's side.

'Bet you're surprised to see me!' he beamed.

'Oh, definitely,' wobbled Marina, suddenly showing extreme interest in her piece of salmon, clumsily mangling its fragile flesh with her blunt knife.

'Your teacher came by the shop at lunchtime and begged me to pop by for a lesson. I've been helping at your mum's store all weekend, it feels like we've barely seen each other! I told her I'd be back in time to close up, but maybe we can plan some investigations this week? We could have a look in the harbour—'

Marina's knife slipped in surprise, tearing a chunk of flesh from her fillet and flinging it across the room, where it hit Wendy in the back, who howled in outrage and spun around to look for the culprit. Marina was suddenly reminded of the night she first met William – her head felt woozy with guilt at the information that she was keeping to herself. Theories continued to tumble about inside her brain, spinning like a loaded washing machine. Everything was linked, she was sure, but how? Someone had thrown

William into the freezing sea without a second's pause, and after thirteen long years they were *still* desperate to cover it up. What else might they have been driven to for the purpose of keeping their secret?

It was all becoming too much for her to bear alone.

'William,' she started, swallowing hard as her tummy turned itself inside out. 'I have to tell you—'

But she was interrupted, this time by the school bell, which burst into life with a sharp buzz that reverberated inside Marina's already fragile head.

'Hold that thought, I should get to the shop!' said William as he jumped to attention. 'And you should get home, you look a little pale . . . Which says a lot coming from me!'

Marina sank into her chair, the moment now passed, and watched her friend bounce blissfully towards the classroom door – star-struck schoolchildren trailing in his wake – as eight grey tentacles nodded in time.

CHAPTER TWENTY-TWO
Extract of European Eel

'Marina, are you sure everything is OK?' asked Edie as they fled the classroom and bounded out into the gloomy afternoon. She placed a palm on her friend's forehead, which felt clammy and cold. 'Let's stop by the Pharma-Sea and ask Mrs Pike to look you over.'

'We really don't have to,' interrupted Marina.

'It's fine, it's practically on the way home,' Edie

pressed as she pulled an empty glass bottle from her bag. 'Plus, I promised I'd post a letter for my mum.'

The Pharma-Sea was tucked away towards the end of Water Lane, where the many fishmongers began to disperse and the buildings faded from shiny glass shopfronts to wind-battered houses that stretched round the narrow cliff paths. Edie and Marina paused as they passed the seafront and began to cross the short stone bridge at the mouth of the harbour.

'Hold on,' Edie panted as she rummaged in her school bag and drew out a thick white envelope. She pulled a cork from the mouth of the glass bottle, which was still held tightly under her arm, and stuffed the letter down its neck. Marina watched as it slowly unfurled inside, revealing an address in the neat handwriting of Edie's mother. Edie replaced the cork with supreme effort, muttering a few choice curse words at the difficulty. Then she lifted her arm and hurled the bottle high into the sky before joining Marina at the edge of the bridge to watch it land in the waves of the harbour with a satisfying splash.

'Who is it for?' Marina asked, watching as the bottle bobbed away in the water towards the open sea.

'It's a letter for my grandma. Mum wants to know if she's coming to stay for Christmas,' Edie replied. 'It should get there in time,' she shrugged, as the girls walked past The Laughing Trout and away from the harbour.

'That reminds me,' Edie said abruptly. 'Are you completely sure that your granny can't remember anything helpful about William?'

Marina gulped as she attempted to retain a blank expression.

'No. It was a complete waste of time,' she fibbed. She didn't want to lie to Edie, but Marina was scared of what saying the truth aloud would mean, as well as the thought of the sympathetic expression she could already imagine forming on her best friend's face.

'That's a shame. You seemed pretty convinced she might hold the key to unlocking this whole mystery.'

'Yeah, it doesn't look like it,' Marina sighed as they arrived at the chemist, her head buzzing louder than ever with thoughts, theories and confusion as the shop door dinged open.

The pungent scent of antiseptic, strong and sterile, hit them square in the face as the smell of the Pharma-Sea's freshly disinfected floor tiles found its way into their noses. A long polished counter ran the length of the narrow shop, behind which were several tall shelves stacked with Perspex boxes of ointments, powders, pills and other medicines. Suddenly, Meredith Pike appeared from below the bench, her brown hair piled on top of her head and held in place by a cuttlefish-bone brooch.

'Why, hello, girls.' She squinted at them from behind a white pair of glasses shaped like cats' eyes.

'Hello, Mrs Pike,' replied Edie. 'Marina has felt a little unwell today. We thought you might have something that could help.'

The pharmacist surveyed Marina suspiciously over the rim of her glasses, which slid clumsily down her long, bumpy nose. 'You are looking quite pale,' she said.

'Um, thanks,' grumbled Marina. 'I think I'm probably OK, actually.'

'Don't listen to her,' Edie interrupted. 'She's looked as though she might be sick all day.'

'Interesting,' mused Meredith, pursing her lips and removing her glasses in thought. 'Well, I'm sure we can find something to help settle your stomach.'

She turned and began to peruse the shelves behind

the counter with a bony finger, her eyelashes fluttering against the Perspex boxes like sticky black moths as she read the labels closely.

'I've a bottle of powdered pufferfish that will have you fighting fit in no time.'

'Pufferfish?' asked Edie, unconvinced.

'Oh, yes, two capsules with dinner would be the perfect pick-me-up.'

'I don't know,' said Marina with a furrowed brow.

'OK,' the pharmacist replied with a whiff of offence, returning to the shelves. She pulled a ladder from the corner of the shop that juddered down a metal track, fixed to the tops of the shelves. 'I might have something else,' she said, climbing to the fifth row of jars, bottles and plastic containers.

'Edie,' whispered Marina. 'You know, I really feel fine.'

'You've not been yourself all day, Marina. You usually won't stop talking about Halloween! You might be coming down with flu. Better to be on top of it early,' Edie said with a nod.

'Here we are!' screeched Mrs Pike in delight, sliding down the sides of the ladder on the arches of her feet. 'Catfish whiskers, known to have many healing properties. One whisker taken with a shot of whisky will help to soothe all kinds of afflictions.'

'I'm not sure Mrs Minnow would be very keen on the whisky,' jabbed Edie.

'You know, you're probably right,' frowned Meredith. 'Wait, I've got something even better!' she cheered, dropping below the counter and rummaging inside a cabinet that was out of sight. Struggling under the weight of a large spigot jar, the pharmacist slowly hoisted the container on to the bench. Inside, a thick grey liquid rolled slowly around the glass with a sickly slither, clinging momentarily to whichever side it sploshed up against.

'Extract of European eel!'

'What has been extracted, exactly?' asked Marina, eyes wide in horror.

'Probably best not to know,' said Meredith. 'But if you think I'm unqualified to prescribe you the right medicine then I'm sure your friend William could rustle up a home remedy. I hear he's quite the authority on fish,' she huffed, clearly irritated.

'You know what,' Marina gasped, the harsh neon lighting of the shop making her vision wobble. 'I think I actually *might* be sick.'

She ran out of the Pharma-Sea, striding up the cliff path away from the town as her eyes adjusted to the dull sky of the late afternoon. Thick grey clouds rolled across the multicoloured rooftops that slid down the hill, heavy with rain that threatened to pour forth at any moment. Marina took several deep breaths of the crisp autumn breeze to steady herself before closing her eyes. Edie appeared at her side, panting from the quick ascent.

'Mrs Pike insisted I bring you a bottle,' she said, holding up a small vial of gooey grey liquid. 'What's going on, Marina? Ever since we found that chest you've been acting so strangely, and whenever someone mentions William it's as if you've seen a ghost. When he showed up at school today, I thought you were going to pass out!'

Marina's head continued to froth as thoughts of baby blankets and old tin cans swirled in her mind's eye. The photo album in her bag seemed to pulse like a dull heart. She looked up to meet the interrogating glare of Edie, who was standing with arms folded in confusion as her billowy black hair fanned behind her in the wind.

'Is there something you're not telling me?' she

urged, holding Marina's gaze with a concerned but unwavering stare.

'It's my dad,' Marina sighed at last, feeling some of the weight on her shoulders lighten, as though the breeze that tickled her neck was lifting part of the guilt she had carried all weekend. 'The fisherman William is looking for is my dad.'

CHAPTER TWENTY-THREE

The Reverential Federation of Fishmongers

Halloween night was a frosty one, as an autumn chill finally gripped the coast with the promise of winter, but the cold alone could not stop the children of the town taking to the streets for trick or treating. Over a dozen home-made William costumes ran up and down the seafront, their cardboard pincers clacking and foam tentacles swinging as colourful leaves blew around their feet. They mingled with sea monsters, mermaids, hammerhead sharks, glowing angler fish and a smattering of sailor ghosts who wore wigs of green seaweed that cascaded down their backs. They banged on doors and screamed in delight as streams of toilet paper flew through the night sky, each child swinging a plastic crabbing bucket which overflowed with tins of candied herring, jellied eels and chocolate-covered clams.

The windows of the Mullet Over fishmonger were boarded shut, Harold Mole having anticipated a night filled by feral, sugar-fuelled children. But that alone couldn't put off a gang of five young boys, each one dressed as a dirty white seagull, from creeping up to the shopfront and hammering on the doors with their feathered fists.

'*Kee-oh!*' cried one. 'Let us in, Harold. *Kee-oh!*'

'Let us have a bite on your scalp. *Kee-oh!*' jeered another. The boys ran in circles in front of the building, screaming and crowing as they flapped the scruffy wings of their costumes, pretending to peck at an imaginary Harold.

'GET BATTERED!' came Harold's booming voice from deep within the building. He slammed the door to his cavernous stock room and turned back to the long table that stretched from one side of the room to the other. Lining the walls, towering shelves crammed full of glass jars displayed an impressive array of preserved fish, from skate to fathead sculpin, while an enormous stuffed blue marlin hung from the ceiling like a monstrous mascot.

The room was packed with people. The Reverential Federation of Fishmongers had gathered for their final meeting ahead of the weekend's annual bonfire celebrations – a spectacular evening of fireworks, fish-finger baps and a huge beacon on the beach. It was the most important festival in Merlington's calendar, marking the journey of larger cod and bass as they passed the coast on their way to their winter spawning grounds . . . Or at least, that's what Harold had *said* would be on the agenda. He cleared his throat with a phlegmy grunt, loudly inviting the chattering fishmongers to be seated.

'Silence,' he called. 'If we could have silence, please. This meeting is called to order.' Chairs were pushed and pulled noisily across the tiled floor, as the other men and women of the Federation attempted to squeeze themselves elbow to elbow around the heavy oak table. Sally Minnow, of course, was never invited for such important and sensitive gatherings, but on this occasion Caroline Carp too was noticeable for her absence.

'What's this all about, Harold?' asked Shrimpy, scratching his long, bony chin as he took a seat next to Walter Whitby, whose presence provoked mild suspicion. 'I thought we'd sorted all the plans for the bonfire.'

Harold squeezed a particularly large dollop of fish oil into his palm, before running it through his repulsive locks. 'We have, Shrimpy. At least, everything you need to worry about. And, Cheryl, no need to be taking minutes – we won't want this on record.'

'No minutes?' blurted Cheryl Shoal, owner of Water Lane's tiny Clam Baked. She tucked her pen behind an ear in disappointment and drummed her turquoise nails on the table. 'Then what have you dragged us here for? I should be at the shop practising my maki rolls. I just can't get the seaweed to wrap tightly enough,' she tutted. 'I don't know what I'm doing wrong.'

'The way I see it is you got t'put pressure on the roll from all three sides at once,' replied Deirdre

Bream, who ran The Codfather at the cliffs end of the high street. 'If you want t'roll it tight, then you've got t'tighten it from the ends an' into the centre all at once.'

'The point is, we wouldn't have to be making all this maki if it weren't for Minnow's and their walking, talking wonder fish,' said Alan Thropp.

'That's right!' interrupted his twin brother Ian, who sat beside him in a mirror image of blonde beard and tortoiseshell glasses. 'They're destroying our business, there's no two ways about it. No one appreciates the art of shucking clams any more . . .'

'Nor the delicacy of our scallops!' added Alan.

Sole Brothers, like every fishmonger's in Merlington, had quickly abandoned their speciality offering to try their hand at rolling sushi and slicing sashimi in an effort to entice back those customers now besotted with William and Minnow's. All but Harold and the Mullet Over, of course, though he'd failed in his efforts to forbid the managers of his other stores from following suit – each had begun flogging their own sashimi too. Caroline Carp, meanwhile, had barely lifted the shutters that covered the entrance of the Carp-e Diem all weekend. She could often be spotted loitering in front of the Minnow's front window with a pensive frown, seizing every opportunity to pop inside and sample whichever sashimi William was serving at that particular moment.

'You've hit the nail on the head there, boys,' declared Harold. 'This tomfoolery has gone on for too long, and something needs to be done. Now. Before this freak show goes national and we become the laughing stock of the entire fishing community.'

While local news outlets had been obsessed with William from the moment he'd washed up – the *Merlington Echo* had even managed to dig up William's supposed 'long-lost sister', a squid they claimed could communicate via blinks – so far, the news had not spread further than a few villages over. No one in the rest of the country took any notice of barmy fishing towns like Merlington, after all, nor their local news reports on the rising costs of motor-boat licences and the overfishing of cod.

Cheryl Shoal scoffed, nevertheless. 'Well, what do you propose we do about it exactly, Harold?'

'I'm not really one for confrontation m'self,' said Deirdre.

'I've got an idea,' interrupted Shrimpy with

exaggerated enthusiasm and a toothy smile. 'Let's just chop the kid up and share out the meat! Problem solved. Some calamari for Sole Brothers, a claw for one of Clam Baked's famous broths and fish fillets for the rest of us!'

As the other fishmongers laughed along with Shrimpy, Harold looked between their merry faces, his eyes narrowing. The shadow of a smirk forming at the corners of his mouth threatened to betray his excitement. He jabbed Walter sharply in the side, signalling his moment to speak.

'Sounds like a plan to me,' the landlord smiled, his blackened lips coated by a mouthful of watery tobacco.

CHAPTER TWENTY-FOUR

The Prime Warden's Plot

*T*he laughter ceased in an instant and a deafening silence enveloped the room, which seemed to darken as though the lights themselves had been dimmed.

'What you on about, Walter?' muttered Deirdre Bream, nervously picking at a crumb of seaweed caught under her nail. 'You can't be serious?'

Michael Undertow, who ran the Undertow

Takeaway opposite Deirdre's high-street shop and spent much of the day admiring her from his grease-coated window, reassured her.

'Don't you mind him, Deirdre. He just likes playing the big man, everyone knows it.'

'I know you don't attend many of these meetings, Walter,' Cheryl Shoal chimed in. 'But we're not in the business of murdering people. That's not exactly in the constitution of the Reverential Federation of Fishmongers, is it? Murder?' She chuckled pointedly, revealing several teeth stained with pink lipstick.

As Cheryl's question hung in the air, the room slowly began to relax at the absurdity of Walter's suggestion. Murder! Over some soggy sashimi and Harold's damaged pride! Deirdre giggled. The rest of the fishmongers' low laughter soon echoed about the cavernous storeroom, bouncing off the glass jars that lined the walls like a ghoulish theatre of pickled prisoners. The absurdly warped faces of countless undying fish looked down on the table.

'It wouldn't be murder, though, would it?' barked Walter, startling the room again. 'The kid's a fish. A flippin' fish that's takin' all of your flippin' fishin' business! Now that's somethin' to laugh about.' He cleared his nose with a stomach-churning snort and spat the tobacco he'd been chewing into a clear glass. It slid down the insides like the clotted black ink of a poorly octopus. 'Because of 'im, my pub's a flippin' ghost town. Looks to me like Catch of the Day don't cut it no more. Murder . . . Ha! What's murderin' a fish to a bunch of flippin' fishmongers?'

The room fell still as the Federation members' eyes darted from one fishmonger to the next, seeking reassurance.

'But what is he?' asked Ian Thropp. 'Is he a fish? Or . . .'

'Is he a boy?' finished his brother Alan.

'Have you ever seen a boy like that before?' mumbled Michael Undertow, scratching a nervous rash that was developing on his forearm.

'Michael!' choked Deirdre in surprise. 'What you sayin'?'

'I'm saying maybe Walter's right. We can't carry on like we have been these last couple o' days. I'm no good with my hands, and I've not got the stomach for this new-fandangled trend for eating raw fish.'

'All right. We're with Shrimpy,' said Alan Thropp.

'Cut him up, share out the fish,' added Ian.

'Hold on now,' blurted a panic-stricken Shrimpy. 'I was only joking! Walter's the one who took me serious.'

A movement of hands and heads began to ripple around the table and a cacophony of frantic murmurs, excited and outraged in equal measure, rose up to the ceiling and the blue marlin which loomed over them. The great beast was encircled by an animated hum of chatter, vibrations jangling up the heavy chains that held it aloft.

'Harold, talk some sense into them,' pleaded Cheryl.

Attention turned to Harold and, with more than a dozen people focused on him, he was in his element. He had watched the debate flare with eager eyes, chomping on a fistful of crabsticks, as taramasalata dripped from his chin. He had searched the assembled fishmongers' faces for every hint of a smile and every stray bead of sweat, judging their reaction to Walter's proposal before making his play.

'Ignore my hungry friend here,' Harold laughed, patting Walter on the back with a weighty hand. 'He lets his imagination run wild sometimes! Murdering a fish, I mean, honestly.'

The landlord quietly seethed in his seat, realizing his suggestion had allowed Harold to save face in front of the crowd at his own expense.

'He's got one thing right, though,' continued Harold forcefully. 'It's a fish. A great, slimy, ruddy big *fish*. Getting up to cod knows what for all that time, out there at the bottom of the English Channel. Washing up on our shore, to spite us and our community.

'He's fast destroying everything we've built and if we don't put a stop to it, we'll be ridiculed by the entire country when this gets out . . . By the rest of the world! Not to mention what it'll do to our livelihoods, our businesses! They're being destroyed by our own disloyal customers and their sick desire for a side of freak show with their fishing produce purchases.

'And you've all seen those claws, we don't know what's going on in that creature's head . . . Imagine the damage they'd do if one day he decided he didn't fancy using them to chop up his fishy old mates any more. I for one am not going to stand by and let Sally Minnow put our futures, our very *lives*, at risk!

'This Federation means the world to me, and as Prime Warden it is my duty to protect our interests.

That means we have but one option – the boy needs to go. Far away from Merlington, and for good.'

'And how are you going to make sure that happens, eh, Harold?' asked Michael Undertow, his rash now a deep crimson.

'I don't want no part in it,' Deirdre cried, grabbing Cheryl Shoal's arm for reassurance.

Harold knew that he needed to tread lightly.

'None of you have to lift a finger, I assure you. Walter and I will take care of everything – we'll just give him enough of a scare that he knows his place is out at sea and *not* here. But I need to know that you're all with me.'

The fishmongers once again broke into muted discussion among themselves. Harold's shirt grew damp as he left them to mutter for a few moments longer, before quickly growing impatient and shoving six crabsticks into his mouth.

'Have you all decided?' he spluttered, showering Walter in spittle as he looked from one fishmonger to the next. His eyes scanned the faces which lined the long table, and each gave him a solemn nod of confirmation. When he came to Deirdre Bream, she paused for a moment, still considering.

'Deirdre?'

'We're with you, Harold,' she said at last, with a hint of unease.

'Then it's settled,' Harold guffawed, his black eyes glowing strangely in the lamplight. 'We need never speak of this meeting again. If anyone should ask, you were here tonight to discuss the bonfire celebrations and *nothing* more.'

'Well, we 'ave been discussin' the bonfire celebration, though, 'aven't we?' Walter said, giving a loud snigger. Harold clipped him around the back of the head.

'What does he mean by that?' asked Shrimpy, as the scraping of chair legs came to an abrupt halt. Each fishmonger was looking to Harold and Walter with curiosity and concern.

'Don't you worry your heads about that. The less you know about our plans, the better it will be for everyone.'

Harold began to reapply his putrid hair ointment, while Walter's gaunt face stiffened into a disconcerting sneer. The rest of the fishmongers rose from the table, content in the knowledge that they were definitely safer knowing as little about the Prime Warden's plot as possible.

'So what does this mean, Harold?' Walter asked, when they were finally alone. 'We're just gonna scare 'im off? The rest of the plan's been cancelled?' The disappointment in his voice was palpable.

'Of course not,' Harold said triumphantly, permitting his lips to stretch into a broad smile. 'You know that I'd never let a good piece of fish go to waste.'

CHAPTER TWENTY-FIVE

Sneeze Guard

$\mathcal{M}$arina was miserable. The novelty of a real-life adventure, which had started just a short time ago, was quickly spiralling into a painful exercise in avoiding *everyone*. She left for school the moment she woke up and did not return home until dinner was on the table, not that she'd been doing any extra school-work. In fact, Marina had been concentrating even less than usual, and on Thursday afternoon, when she was asked by Mrs Orr how best to remove a squid's ink sac, she was sent to the head teacher's office for suggesting you 'just give it a tickle'.

Marina's relief after sharing Granny Minnow's story with Edie had been short-lived. It had done nothing for her investigation, except instil in her an overwhelming sense of dread. It ticked away like a bomb in the pit of her stomach all week – counting down to what, she did not know. Not only did she feel as though she needed to have some more concrete answers before telling William her discovery, the thought of being the one to break his heart with the truth was once again unbearable. Nigel Minnow had been lost at sea for years and he probably wasn't coming back, no matter how many stories of his epic survival she dreamt up.

I can lie to myself all I like, she thought despondently. *But I can't stretch my hope wide enough for the both of us.*

The trail had grown cold. They were still no closer to finding out who was behind the mysterious trunk dumped in the sea, despite Edie's attempts to bribe the harbour master for details on any recent movements of midnight motorboats. All they knew was that whoever had been cruel enough to hurl a defenceless baby into the English Channel was still trying to cover up the act to this day. Marina was certain that the chest of clothes and toys had once been William's, abandoned in the sea by the same person who continued to try and sink their secrets to the ocean floor. Even more alarming, she was beginning to suspect that her father may have met a similar fate...

The fisherman had warned William that it wasn't safe to bring him on land. If someone was *so* desperate to keep their connection to him a secret, was it really that far-fetched to think they might have had a hand in Nigel Minnow's disappearance as well?

The longer Marina allowed the week to whizz by, the more exposed she felt, and the more it seemed impossible to share any of her unhappy findings. Would the knowledge put her mother in danger too? Was William *still* in danger? All of these thoughts and more threatened to pop her head like a pimple, and left her feeling closer than ever to breaking point.

On the morning of the bonfire, Marina found herself unable to wriggle out of helping behind the counter at Minnow's. Business was still booming, as crowds continued to cram inside the bustling walls, desperate to feed their thirst for sliced sashimi and to ogle the peculiar boy with scales.

At least it's too busy for Mum or William to carry on questioning me, Marina thought with a sigh of relief. She'd been so miserable lately; they were certain to know something was wrong. Unfortunately, her peace of mind was short-lived. At four o'clock, Sally began to close the shop early as the whole of Merlington ground to a halt ahead of the evening's celebrations.

'Marina, thank you for your help today,' Sally cooed. 'You two can run off while I finish up. Why don't you get on with some investigations since you've both a bit of free time?'

'That's OK, Mum,' Marina instantly replied, hell-bent on avoiding being alone with William. She scanned the room frantically, searching for an escape. 'I should clean the sneeze guards; they're looking really gross.'

Sally feigned fainting in shock as she held a blue plastic-gloved hand to her forehead.

'You want to clean the sneeze guards? My daughter, who left a bowl of clam chowder in her bedroom for almost a fortnight?'

'Sure,' muttered Marina, looking anxiously over her shoulder at William who was sweeping the tiles in time to 'Big Mouth' Billy Bass. 'You've been so busy lately and I know I've not been a whole lot of help.'

'That's very sweet, Marina, but there's really no need. Why don't you take William down to the beach? He could have a swim out to the buoy and look for this mysterious object you were so keen to find . . . You've been so busy with school this week, and I've taken all of William's time; you should go and have a hunt while you can.'

Marina's heart stopped when she saw William snap to attention at the suggestion. All eight of his tentacles perking up and waving wildly from his scalp in excitement.

'Oh, yes, let's do it, Marina. That would be brilliant,' he beamed.

'No. There's really no time, I've plenty of work to do here.'

'Marina,' urged Sally with a frown. 'I said it's fine. Go with William.'

'But, Mum . . .'

'But nothing. Go with William, and I'll see you this evening at the bonfire.'

William placed a claw on the small of Marina's back and began to lead her towards the door. She dug her feet in, trying to scrub the front of the counter as she was pulled through the store on her heels, leaving a long snail-like streak across the glass in the process.

'William, no . . . The sneeze guards, I need to . . .' she spluttered, trying to break free from the oblivious boy who smiled happily as he opened the door. 'William, I said *NO*!'

Marina surprised herself with the outburst, tearing the back of her shirt as she twisted violently away from William's claw. Feeling the rip with the back of her hand, she looked down at the polished floor, a wave of shame washing over her.

'William, I . . .'

He looked between the reddening face of his friend and her mother, whose own face was beginning to colour in anger. 'No, I'm . . . I'm sorry. I thought . . .'

'William,' Sally spoke softly as she tried to control her voice. 'Why don't you have a swim around the bay yourself? We're running low on seaweed and you could keep an eye out for this mysterious object too. I need to speak with my daughter. Alone.'

William gave Marina a confused look as he made

his way towards the door, before disappearing into the sinking sunlight with a delicate ding of the bell.

Sally turned to her daughter. 'Marina, what on earth? How could you speak to William like that? And after being so keen to drag him out into the sea last weekend on this wild hunt. What is going on?'

Marina, drained of energy and completely out of ideas, sighed as she reached behind the counter and into her school bag. To her mother's surprise and puzzlement, she pulled out the Minnow family photo album.

CHAPTER TWENTY-SIX

The Famous William

William wandered down the high street, baffled by Marina's behaviour, but forgiving and excited to have a swim for the first time in ages. The occasional dip from the storeroom jetty couldn't really compete with feeling the weight of the sea, which seemed as if it held him in its palm, the roll of the white waves breaking across his shimmering, scaled back.

While he was happy to finally be visiting dry land, William was keen to continue the hunt for his long-lost fisherman – which began with finding the object that had knocked him out. He was grateful for the warmer than warm welcome he had received from the Minnows, but when he'd pictured starting a new life in Merlington it had always included his father. His mind sailed back to memories of the days and weeks which bled together incoherently, the endless hours spent sitting on his old pile of nets, wondering each time the wind whistled through the rotting old boards of the bait shop whether it was the fisherman returning at last.

'The famous William.' A loud, unexpected voice came from behind, pulling him from his thoughts as he passed The Laughing Trout on his way to the beach. 'It's a pleasure to finally meet you.'

William turned to see two men bearing down on him – one small and weedy with a crooked smile, the other large and glistening with an oily sheen. He smelt just like his old, mouldy bait shop home had on a warm summer's day. Fishy and fungal.

'William, I'm Harold. And this is Walter – the owner of this fine establishment,' the large man said, indicating the pub behind them.

'Hello,' said William politely.

'I'm sorry I've not managed to come to Minnow's and meet you sooner,' started Harold. 'We've been so busy with plans for tonight's bonfire festivities that I've not had the chance.'

'That's quite all right,' said William, eyeing a pair of seagulls that had perched themselves on the wooden pub sign swinging gently above their heads.

'You'll be at the party tonight, then, eh?' asked Walter with a toothy grin.

'Yes, definitely, I'll be there with Mrs Minnow and Marina.'

'Splendid!' boomed Harold. 'We were just on our way to the harbour. We're taking the boat out to catch some last-minute fish for the celebrations. Even with all our planning, I'm concerned we won't have enough food for everyone. You can draw quite the crowd, if you didn't know. Won't you join us?'

'I'm sorry, but I have some seaweed to collect for Mrs Minnow.' He turned and continued on his way towards the sea.

'Oh, you'll be back before she has the chance to notice. It will be so much quicker with the help of a strapping young lad like yourself. You could pick up some seaweed at the same time,' urged Harold.

'I'm sorry, no. I have to get going,' said William, beginning to feel uneasy. Something was strange about the pair's keen interest in him. He noticed the smaller one was making sure to keep a beady eye on his claws. He carried on walking, across the harbour bridge and down the sloping promenade towards the water which shimmered in the low sun.

Suddenly Harold was in the way once again. Sensing that the opportunity was slipping away, he grabbed hold of William's shoulder, gritting his teeth to mask the repulsion he felt at making contact with the scaly skin.

'I'm sure your father would help us,' he said quietly. 'He is such a generous man.'

William stopped abruptly in his tracks as the two seagulls leapt from their wooden perch and swooped, colliding on either side of Harold's greasy head.

'What did you say?' he asked, spinning around as Harold fought off the birds with clenched, burly fists. 'You know my dad? The fisherman?'

Harold had one gull by its legs as he swung it into the sky like a hammer throw. Walter chased the other, hurling pieces of bait at its bottom, which only attracted more birds, snapping at his ankles with sharp beaks.

'Oh, yes,' spluttered Harold, trying to regain some composure. 'I know him very well. I would've loved to talk to you about him, but we really must be getting on. It was lovely to have met you.'

William looked back up the high street towards the Minnow's shopfront, the road completely deserted now except for the postman, who had emerged from the harbour in full scuba-diving gear – a sack of soaking wet glass bottles clanging behind him.

No one would miss him, for just a short time.

'Wait,' said William. 'I'll come with you.'

'Marvellous,' boomed Harold, running a fresh fist-ful of oil through his revolting mane as he recovered from the seagull attack. 'Then let's make haste.'

Harold put an arm around William's shoulder with as much delicacy as he could muster, and after he had shared a sneering smile with Walter, the two men made their way around the stone breakwater towards the harbour entrance, their new companion in tow.

A short while later, the sea rippled like a lump of

jellied eels tapped with a spoon as Harold's speedboat raced through the water, the emblem of the Mullet Over emblazoned on its sides. The passengers made a peculiar trio as the sun slowly dipped beneath the horizon – early even for a November night. Harold took up two-thirds of the boat himself, and his great shadow cast a long and ominous shape on the dark water. Walter, with his scraggly arms and spindly fingers, kept a tight grip on the speedboat's tiller and guided them shakily away from land. Sandwiched between them, like a sardine squished in the tin, was the strange boy with the luxurious head of tentacles.

'You said you know my father,' urged William over the trembling noise of the engine. He had thought until now that Harold couldn't quite hear him, so raised his voice appropriately (while always maintaining politeness). 'Is that true? Do you know where he went?'

Harold turned to Walter with a nod, and the landlord cut the boat's engine. The sudden silence was deafening as William realized just how far they'd come from land.

'You want to know about your father?' asked Harold, his smile of contempt lost on the boy, who was blinded by excitement.

'Yes! Please,' exclaimed William, standing up sharply in his enthusiasm for knowledge. 'Absolutely anything you might know that could help me find him.'

He didn't feel the pain of Walter's wooden oar striking him across the back of the head until he was face down on the floor of the boat.

'Which father do you mean?' gloated Harold. 'The one who hid you in the bait shop before he met his untimely end? Or the one who threw you back into the sea as a baby, without a second glance?'

William rubbed the back of his head, massaging a particularly bruised tentacle as all eight throbbed from Walter's wallop. 'What ... what are you doing?'

'What I should have done thirteen years ago!' Harold's eyes gleamed, victory visible in every fold of his face. 'You were meant to have sunk back to the depths where you belong, but that meddling fisherman had to go and stick his oar in. Well, he's not here to save you this time, and I'll make sure the job is done properly!'

William pulled himself to his feet as Walter once again swung the oar, cracking him across the side of the head with another sickening squelch. His skull pounded. He staggered in confusion, tripping on his own feet and falling backwards over the side of the boat into the sea.

'No!' he heard Harold shriek, the fishmonger's voice losing its composure in an instant. William floated face down in the water, groggy but listening intently. He heard Harold throw himself to the side of the boat, dangerously rocking the tiny vessel and causing waves to wash over his still-throbbing tentacles. 'Hurry up and grab an arm! Don't let him swim away!'

'I can't get a flippin' grip,' Walter yelled, as William allowed his wet and scaly limb to slip woozily through the publican's fist like a limp eel.

Suddenly he felt a second, more powerful hand wrap around one of his own enormous claws. He sensed his body moving through the water – pulled towards the boat by Harold's formidable strength. Reacting on instinct and fuelled by fear, he sprang to life and with his other free arm grabbed hold of Harold's meaty shoulder with a sharp pincer.

'Arggghhh!' cried Harold in shock, dropping William's other claw as he fell backwards into the bow of the boat. The tentacle boy sank beneath the water, disappearing into the night.

Harold clutched his shoulder, sucking a pudgy thumb to console himself.

'Umm, Harold?' said Walter, whose presence the fishmonger had completely forgotten.

'What?' he barked, tearing his thumb from his lips in embarrassment.

''E's gone.'

'What?'

''E's swum off. I s'pose that's what fish do, ain't it? Swim off places,' he groaned.

Harold scanned the eerily calm sea for any sign of movement.

'Fishsticks,' he sighed.

'Well, what we gonna do, eh, Harold? You promised me one of them claws for my Catch of the Day! What am I s'posed to do for the pub's Sunday lunch now?'

Harold's mind whirred as he formulated their next move.

'It's OK,' he said, looking down at the tiny bloodstain forming on the collar of his torn white shirt. 'We can work with this.'

'But what if 'e's gone ashore?' asked Walter. 'If 'e tells 'em I hit 'im, that'll be it for me!'

Harold looked across to the distant coastline, where blinking lights signalled the gathering bonfire crowds beginning to pour on to Merlington's seafront.

'He won't go back,' Harold muttered, almost to himself. He motioned for Walter to start the engine. 'This time he can't come back.'

'*This* time?' asked Walter, more confused than ever as he set their boat on course for the abandoned old pier which swayed in the distance.

'THIS TIME,' Harold screamed into the night, 'HE WON'T DARE COME BACK!'

CHAPTER TWENTY-SEVEN

Harold's Story

*H*arold Mole was famous. Well, he was as famous as you could be in a town as small as Merlington. Born to Morris and Helga Mole one ordinary autumn morning, Harold caused his family to become an overnight sensation when he set the British record for being the largest *ever* baby, weighing an eye-watering 15lb 9oz. On the front page of the following day's *Merlington Echo*, you'd have been justly forgiven for mistaking Mr and Mrs Mole as having posed for a photo with their favourite pink beach ball, rather than their newborn son.

Baby Harold's appetite was unrivalled. So great that milk alone would never have been enough to satisfy him and at three weeks old, with Helga Mole at her wits' end, Harold was happily chowing down on liquidized lobster and a bedtime bottle of boiled clam chowder. As the baby quickly grew on this unusual diet, so too did his meals. Before long Harold would refuse an afternoon nap without first having a hefty helping of minced crabmeat, and the only way to end his insufferably loud crying (his lungs were almost as large as his stomach) would be to wave a cleaned-out claw in his face, which he'd suck on furiously like some kind of fishy pacifier.

Once he started to teethe, it seemed like the only way to soothe the sorry boy's pain was a horrid fish paste, which his father would rub into his gums wearing a surgical-grade mask to disguise the putrid smell. Not only that, soon the toddler developed a scaly dry skin condition that his parents treated twice daily with a bath of omega-3 oils which he loved beyond anything. He'd swirl around the tub of glistening, multicoloured water like a plump seal, emerging an hour later relieved of his psoriasis, stinking of ammonia and hungry for yet another meal.

After starting at school, Harold flew to the top of his class (because who else would know that a lungfish could live to be sixty-five years old?) and was destined for great things in a town as mad about seafood as Merlington. His appetite, though, only grew with him and he would spend even his favourite class, The History of Fishmongering, chomping on crabsticks and taramasalata.

'You'll turn into a fish one of these days,' Helga Mole would cry, as she piled his dinner plate with a third helping of fried calamari, breaded fish or yet another bowl of lobster bisque. Harold paid her no mind, continuing to fill his bottomless stomach with fish as fat as a porpoise.

At nineteen, his luscious blond locks beginning to thin, Harold started applying a rancid ointment of his own concoction in an attempt to retain some form of a hairstyle. While the seagulls in town delighted in his foul-smelling forehead, the people of Merlington felt quite the opposite. It was not until his parents passed away and he joined the Reverential Federation of Fishmongers upon inheriting their store, the Mullet Over, that anyone could bear to be in the same room as him. Mainly because they were *forced* to at meetings of the council.

Harold's monopoly on the town's fishmongers quickly grew from one, to three, to six successful stores and first sight of the local fishermen's catch each morning. He was achieving his goals as quickly as he could make them, so obsessed with his fishy ambitions that life sped by in a blur of salt cod, shop-fronts and shucking oysters. But a great depression soon came over Harold. His daily drum of calamari could no longer please him, and his evening pan of boiling-hot bouillabaisse left him cold. His life was perfect and just as he'd always planned it, and yet he needed more.

Then one day Caroline Carp had breezed through his shop doors. She was like no woman Harold had ever met, with neatly coiffed curls of blonde hair that bounced on her shoulders, a smudge of red lipstick and a deep laugh like a sailor's. Harold was instantly besotted by her charm, wit and work ethic – and the fact that she could reel off an alphabet of exotic fish that even he found impressive. As she ordered six live lobsters (all for herself), drawing a crystal perfume atomizer from her purse and spraying her neck with a foul, fishy fragrance, Harold was overcome by desire and asked her out on a date. The very next day they spent an afternoon crabbing on the beaches of Merlington, competing as they dangled their lines off the stone breakwater that curled around the shore, hoisting their catch from the depths and into a shiny castle-shaped plastic bucket as they each avoided the hungry gulls that dove at them from above.

The months sped by, and with Caroline installed as the manager of one of Harold's six fishmongers, the newly renamed Carp-e Diem, the two were inseparable. Soon after, now living together above the Mullet Over and as close as two people could be, the couple decided to take the next step and begin a family of their own. Harold doted on Caroline, drawing a nightly bath of saltwater collected from the Channel, as she came home each evening with a new toy or outfit that quickly filled an antique chest in the corner of their cosy flat. But, despite a stringent routine of sea sponge scrubs and cod brine belly ointments, no baby appeared and a twosome they remained.

Caroline came to terms with their new reality, throwing herself gladly into her work and the humdrum of daily life, content in the knowledge that they lived a joyful existence. Harold, on the other hand, was furious to be denied the privilege of a child to mould in his own image . . . A *son* to gift with this greatest of legacies, built with his own two hands! His wrath poured into every corner of his life like an oil spill, polluting the very foundations of his happiness. On nightly walks he crashed through the surf, anger sinking his bare feet deep into the wet sand with every step. There wasn't a world in which he didn't see himself with the child he so rightly deserved. He cursed the water, the waves and the sea itself for the hand he had been dealt.

'I have everything that I ever wanted!' he cried in a rage-fuelled fever. 'Yet you mock me, deny me the very thing that could make me truly happy. The *son* I deserve!'

But Harold could never have expected that the sea would send an answer . . .

CHAPTER TWENTY-EIGHT

A Delivery of Squid

Just a few weeks later, as the summer mornings heralded early dawns and earlier sailors, Caroline arrived to open the Carp-e Diem. After haggling over a day's supply of brill, bream and bass with the fishermen gathered at her shop's front door, she lugged her fresh supplies into the storeroom to find an extra item — she'd been left an enormous, brown wooden crate. Sealed shut, but heavy with the weight of a bountiful fisherman's catch.

Pulling back the bulky lid, Caroline was delighted to find a generous supply of delicious fresh squid. Twenty wriggling bodies slid around the bottom of the box, their many tentacles writhing and twisting together with curiosity as they searched for the life-giving water from which they'd been snatched just a few hours earlier.

But then, to her surprise, a face appeared among the suckers. Hidden beneath the squirming grey bodies, a newborn baby, not yet a week old, returned Caroline's gaze. She was overcome by horror and confusion in equal measure. Her arms lunged into the melee as she searched for the baby's slime-covered body before tearing him free from the wriggling pit. But not all of the tentacles fell away.

She knew it was wrong in an instant. Holding the creature in one arm, she pulled the white telephone from the wall and summoned Harold to her side immediately. He crashed through the shop door and Caroline turned towards him. As the short tentacles slipped from her elbow and dangled before his eyes, they were both lost for words. Harold's face fell into a mirror image of his partner's open-mouthed, silent stare. Caroline leant forward and placed the child among the twinkling ice chips of her shop's display cabinet. They looked down in terror at his iridescent body, glittering in the harsh tube lighting; his rubbery scalp bulbous and soft, and writhing still; his small amber pincers in the place of human hands. The child that Harold knew, in that instant, he had wished for.

At first, they went along with things as best they possibly could. They dressed the child in blue cotton babygrows, cutting off the sleeves in order to fit his strange claws through the folds. Caroline rocked him to sleep in an antique cradle, singing him sea shanties as he drifted off to slumber. They acted as though everything was normal, while understanding that nothing was the same.

You'll turn into a fish one day. Harold's mother's words rang in his ears as he looked down at this child the universe had deemed fit to carry on his legacy. Caroline tried her best to convince him that the baby, strange as it was, was a gift – sent to them for a reason. It was happy, loving, warm, and all it seemed to crave was their love in return. But Harold's heart had grown colder by the day, and now sank in his chest as it hardened like stone.

'It's no gift,' he insisted. 'I cursed the sea, and the sea cursed me right back.'

One thing was certain. The baby was a child of the water, and all they had to do was return him to his rightful place. In the ocean he would flourish, find his own way in the sunken world and live the life that they could never provide for him. Under the cover of darkness, Harold would take the boy out to sea and lower him gently into the depths – releasing him from a life of abnormality on land and them of the burden that such a child would bring.

But that was just the start of their troubles. After the horrid deed was done, one dark and stormy August evening, the couple only drifted further apart as a feeling of unbearable guilt grew in Caroline as fast as Harold's resolve strengthened.

'We are monsters,' she said one morning after yet another sleepless night. It was the first time they had spoken to one another in more than a week. Harold looked up from a pitcher of prawn cocktail, his appetite having remained unchanged.

'We've been through this,' he urged across the tentacle-patterned tablecloth. 'We did the right thing, for us as well as the creature.'

'That *creature* was sent to us for a reason,' Caroline shrieked, hot tears beginning to coat her narrow eyes. 'He was our *son*!'

'I told you never to use that word,' Harold bellowed, slamming his fist on the table in fury as his breakfast toppled over and spilt pink mayonnaise across his lap.

'You can bury your head in the seaweed all you like,' hiccoughed Caroline. 'But what we have done is unforgivable.'

She moved out that very afternoon.

The years went by and Harold spared little thought for the son he'd returned to the ocean, happy that life had returned to blissful normality. But one rainy October evening, as he settled down for an after-dinner snack of smoked mackerel bruschetta with a drizzle of cod liver oil, muffled voices drew Harold's attention to the window. Peeling back the living-room curtains, he eyed the pinstripe canvas canopy sheltering the entrance of the Mullet Over. Sitting on a pile of crates was the ghastly Minnow girl, loudly jabbering away to her friend with a ladybird umbrella, about a boy who had the most fantastic claws for hands.

Harold collapsed to the floor with a wheeze, winded by the words that floated down the high street like a ghost come to haunt him. He sat curled in a giant ball for what felt like hours, numb to his emotions and deaf to the television which hummed away cheerfully playing the evening news bulletin. How could this have happened? How could that Minnow girl have discovered the creature he'd fought so hard to forget? Surely it was just a matter of time before someone turned up at his door . . . No. There was no way to connect him to that monster. Caroline would not dare breathe a word of their secret history, and it would be impossible for the creature to have any memory of their wicked deeds.

But the chest had to go. He stared at it now in the corner of the flat, still full of baby clothes and toys for a child he'd supposedly never had. Treasured as a reminder of the happy times he and Caroline had shared, it was now the single most dangerous item to his peaceful existence. The only thing that threatened to incriminate him. Harold looked at the clock above the fireplace, surprised to see that it was half past two in the morning. Possessed with sudden urgency he pulled himself from the floor, threw on a raincoat and hoisted the trunk on to his shoulder. Tearing through the flat and down into the Mullet Over's storeroom, he pulled the trunk on to a small jetty and into his speedboat which bobbed readily in wait. Lumbering on board, he sparked the motor to life and slowly drove out into the moonlight – hopeful that no one would spy him in the darkness, but unable to push down a niggling feeling of déjà vu. The memory of his last midnight harbour dumping, more than thirteen years ago, hovered in the corners of his mind . . .

An hour and a half later, Harold lay awake in bed as he pondered how long it might be before that interfering Minnow girl blabbered any further. If she told anyone else about this most peculiar discovery, it could ruin everything he'd worked so hard to protect. *But the girl is famous for her fibs*, Harold thought. Who would believe her? Her friend with the umbrella certainly hadn't, so she'd be hard pressed to convince the cynics of Merlington.

Little did Harold know at that moment, it would take no effort on Marina's part at all.

CHAPTER TWENTY-NINE

The Photo Album

Sally stood at the counter of her shop, her shocked expression reflected in the wide eyes of the mullet and mackerel slowly spoiling in the display cabinet. Looking up from the photo album she held in her hands was her husband Nigel, smiling in one of the last pictures taken of him before his unexplained disappearance. Despite his weathered features and coarse, greying hair, his brilliant smile and bright teeth gave a hint of the youthful man she had fallen in love with. Now, all Sally could do was question what had been true in those later years. Could Granny Minnow's story, which Marina had just recounted in minute detail, really be genuine? It seemed like the only explanation as to how her befuddled mother-in-law could have possibly known of William's existence. Though had Nigel really been capable of keeping a secret this big from her for so long? They were meant to have been a team. Sally racked her brains, trying to remember where her husband might have said he'd been going all of those times he must have actually been sneaking away to visit his fishy adopted son. All of that extra time that they could have spent as a family ...

'Mum,' started Marina. 'What are we going to do?'

The night was drawing in, and crowds were beginning to float past Minnow's dark shopfront as people made their way to the bonfire celebrations. Marina watched her school friends and neighbours drift along the high street, cosy in their winter coats, some children waving sparklers. A large group of boys ran noisily past the window carrying a spongy mannequin above their heads, ready to be thrown on the fire.

They had crammed several pillows into some old jogging bottoms and a baggy grey sweatshirt. Swinging from the head of the dummy Marina saw eight long tube socks, each sewn to its scalp and stuffed full of feathers.

Sally stirred herself into action.

'First things first, we need to tell William the truth. It's better he knows everything now than finds out later by some other means.'

'But, Mum . . .'

'But nothing, Marina,' Sally snapped. 'It will be kinder coming from us. Sometimes you have to be honest with the people you care about, even though it might hurt them in the process.' She went back once more to the photo album, flicking through the pages before landing on a photo of herself and Nigel. They were sitting together laughing on the bow of his fishing boat, and over her shoulder, the burnt-out pier was visible, rising from the sea like a menacing splodge in the fuzzy background.

'I know you're right,' Marina conceded. 'But how can we do that to him? Tell him . . . that his father probably won't be coming back.'

Sally paused in surprise and looked up at her

daughter, finally seeing the sadness behind her eyes. 'That doesn't sound very much like my Marina,' she said tenderly. 'What happened to a friendly pod of dolphins rescuing Dad from the sea? Or . . . that enormous pelican that scooped him up and carried him away to safety?'

'I don't know,' sighed Marina. 'I've not really been in the mood for dreaming up any more wild stories lately.'

Sally put down the photo album and walked around the Minnow's counter, pulling her daughter gently into a warm embrace that they held for a short while.

'I'm not sure how I'd have made it through the last few years if it hadn't been for all of your brilliant stories,' she sniffed.

Marina failed to suffocate a whimper which escaped from within the folds of her mother's greasy apron. 'I'm just tired of trying to lie to myself . . .'

'Now stop that at once!' Sally barked, breaking from their cuddle to look directly into Marina's eyes. 'Your stories give us *both* hope, and your dad would hate for us to give up on him! Imagine how embarrassed you'll be if he turns up on the beach tomorrow, just as you've stopped inventing tales of his epic survival on the seas.'

'I guess.' Marina smiled half-heartedly to indulge her mother. The recent events had made her feel so much older than her twelve years, prematurely aged by an investigation which only seemed to lead to further confusion and escalating gloom. It had felt like such an adventure on the morning she'd stood on the beach in her pink flippers, ready to solve the riddle of the tentacle boy from the sea. For a moment, it had seemed as though a family reunion could be on the cards – for both of them.

'I'm sorry you've had to deal with this on your own,' Sally started. 'I've let myself get carried away with all of the attention we've been receiving, when I should've been paying attention to you.'

'That's OK, Mum,' Marina smiled. 'You can help me now, as I've no idea where to start.'

'I think our most pressing concern is who this antique trunk might belong to,' mused Sally. 'The owner must have been incredibly desperate if they felt their only option was to hurl it into the sea, the very night you met William, no less. We're backing them into a corner, and I'm worried about how much further they might go in order to keep their involvement a secret.'

'It's the same person that was mean enough to abandon William in the first place! Whoever it was that dumped him in the water and left him for Dad to find at the bottom of his fishing net ... They seem to have a thing for chucking stuff in the sea.' Marina's brow creased in disapproval.

'Do you think they could have ever known that your father uncovered their secret?' Sally asked bleakly.

Marina shrugged. A queasy feeling bubbled in her stomach as she wondered whether her mother would really want to hear her answer . . . That her father's disappearance was linked, she was sure.

They stood in silent contemplation as a sluggish oyster slunk from the ice-filled display cabinet, dragging itself along the glass with an elongated foot at a glacial speed. The loud and urgent ticking of the clock behind the counter suddenly drew Sally's attention.

'It's getting late, what could be taking William so long? I'm anxious that we get all of this out into the open as soon as possible,' she said with a grim determination.

'You don't think something could have happened to him?' asked Marina, panicked. Her question went unanswered and hung in the air on a fog of uncertainty as the sounds of multiple gasps and shouts drifted into the shop – an unexpected din rising like a tidal wave that was sweeping into sight on the horizon.

'That sounds like it's coming from the Mullet Over,' Sally said with a scowl. 'We should probably go and find out what's happening.'

Marina's stomach did a somersault as her whole body, from her earlobes to her toenails, was washed with a feeling of dread. Tearing open the photo album that still lay on the counter, she pulled the last picture taken of Nigel Minnow from its plastic slot before popping it in her pocket and scurrying from the shop behind her mother.

'Your great, flipping, fish friend—' He spoke slowly, savouring the pleasure of the moment.

'William,' interrupted Sally.

'Wil— Whatever you want to call it. That *thing* attacked me.'

'He would never hurt anyone!' screamed Marina, outraged by the suggestion and making several fishmongers beside her jump with surprise.

'Oh, really?' sneered Harold haughtily, looking down his sweaty nose at the girl.

Deirdre piped up, her arms folded. 'It happened, Sally, that feral fish is out of control. Walter was there too, an' saw the whole thing.'

The crowd turned to Walter, who stood on the periphery, chewing tobacco. Harold eyed him with encouragement. Marina was once again on the verge of tears as anger propelled through her body.

'It's true,' choked Walter. 'We took it – 'im – William, that is, out on the boat to catch some fish for the bonfire an' that . . .' He looked to Harold nervously for reassurance. 'An' he says that Minnow's runs things round 'ere now an' that we 'ad to get in line or face . . . face the consequences.'

'Daddy!' cried Wendy Whitby, clutching her

father's side and shooting a look of deep disdain at Marina. 'You were so brave, facing that horrible sea creature all by yourself.'

Walter blushed at his daughter's misplaced pride while Marina quietly seethed, grinding her teeth with such a force that she risked reducing them to powder.

'Come on, Harold,' pleaded Sally, who sensed the turn this was taking. 'This is ridiculous. Everyone here has met William; they all love him! They know he'd never say such a thing.'

'Is that so?' asked Harold gleefully. He began to unbutton the top of his torn shirt, pulling the left collar down to expose a red cut, faint but unmistakably the outline of a very large crab claw.

Marina stared at the wound through watery eyes, attempting to blink back the wetness unsuccessfully.

'You're lying!' she shouted, fixed on Harold as she aimed a trembling hand in his direction, radiating waves of pure loathing.

'You'd know all about lying, wouldn't you, Marina?' spat Wendy, walking to the centre of the mob. 'Everyone knows that you're full of it, talking a load of rubbish and *always* telling lies to get attention. You'd say absolutely anything to protect that fishy freak.'

Marina's ears burnt red and her legs wobbled with wooziness.

'I am *not* a liar!' she cried. 'William is the sweetest boy I've ever met, I just—'

'Oh my cod, look at her top!' interrupted Cheryl Shoal wildly, pointing a quivering, lacquered finger at Marina's back. The crowd turned to see the small tear of fabric at the bottom of her shirt, exploding as one with noise at the sight.

'That thing has hurt the girl too!' shrieked Goldie Harrison.

'No!' pleaded Marina, in between sobs.

'It's got to be stopped!' yelled the Thropp brothers in perfect unison.

'You've got it all wrong, please!'

'The poor girl, it's brainwashed her!' bawled Cheryl.

'It was a misunderstanding...'

'Marina,' started Harold, feasting on the excitement that was brewing inside of him. 'You're safe with us, we can protect you. Just give up this monster before it has the chance to hurt anyone else.'

'He didn't . . . He hasn't . . .' spluttered Marina, backing through the feverish crowd, away from the terrifying situation unravelling.

'I believe the girl,' came a voice. Caroline Carp appeared among the commotion. 'That boy wouldn't hurt a fly, and all of you know it. He's much more than just a fish.'

Harold stared daggers at the woman he'd once loved, knowing that the guilt she had nurtured in secret for thirteen years now fuelled her.

'And why would anyone care what you had to say, eh, Caroline? Hanging around that Minnow's place like some sixteen-year-old fangirl.'

A nearby group of giggling teenagers, eavesdropping on the argument, immediately zipped up their coats to hide the William-branded T-shirts beneath.

'Don't test me,' Caroline warned, returning Harold's gaze with sharp eyes and a steely resolve.

'I think you need some time off,' he threatened. 'Close Carp-e Diem for a while, you've earnt yourself a holiday. Perhaps a nice boat trip, there's an idea . . .'

Caroline's face turned pink as she wrinkled her brow at the hidden warning, before turning and disappearing through the throng of people still huddled tightly watching the drama unfold.

'Everyone needs to calm down,' begged Sally.

'There is a simple explanation for all of this, I just know it.'

Harold guffawed, loving every second of the chaos he had created. 'Oh? Then how do you explain this?' He pulled once again on the collar of his shirt to shouts from the crowd.

Marina continued to back away from the horde, suddenly finding herself standing beneath the neon sign of Sole Brothers at the edge of the beach. Her face was illuminated by the electric blue of two flashing Dover sole (or were they lemon sole?) as she watched the angry mob pulsate with gesturing arms and shaking heads. Unable to think, and desperate to be far from the booming voices debating her innocent friend's fate, she found herself running. She dashed through the early bonfire crowds and across the wooden groynes that rose from the exposed sand of low tide like strings of fat, gnarly thumbs. She tore down the beach as it sloped away from town, the cliffs towering over her, and let the lights and the angry voices fade away.

What had she started that first evening? When she'd rowed out to the old pier and met William – the most amazing person she had ever laid eyes on. Could she have ever foreseen this? And if she had, would she have turned her boat around and left him alone to his quiet safety? Perhaps if she had been honest with William from the moment they had found that antique chest, then right now they would all be sitting around the dinner table planning their next move. Instead she'd left her mother to pacify a town of seventeen fishmongers who were probably planning a hunt for him at this very moment. For all she knew, he had been hurt by Harold already. There was nothing else for it. Marina would have to find him, and find him quickly. Warn him not to come home . . .

But where would he be?

CHAPTER THIRTY-ONE

Back to the Pier

A cold wind blew Marina's hair from behind, sending a violent shiver down her spine as she looked out to sea and laid eyes on the old pier rocking on its precarious stilts, far offshore.

Would he have gone back there, she thought, *where it all began?*

'Marina, are you all right?' called Edie, rushing along the beach beside Thea – both girls panting in their friend's wake. They were wrapped in cosy woollen coats, ready for the bonfire celebrations, Thea clutching a thermos of pumpkin spiced tea.

'We're with you, Marina,' she chirped from inside her fuzzy hood. 'We know William would never have hurt you, he's way too nice to ever do that.'

'And who wouldn't take a swipe at Harold if they had the chance?' Edie chuckled, raising her fists for a mock fight. 'Can you believe all the fuss he was making over such a tiny little scratch?'

'There *was* a lot of blood. It made me feel a bit woozy.'

'It was probably just a load of watered-down ketchup,' said Edie, batting away Thea's concern. 'I'm only surprised that he would be willing to waste good food.'

The girls laughed, but Marina barely heard them. Instead she stared across the water to the pier, her mind whirring with worry as a plan finally popped into existence.

'I need you both to run back to the high street and fetch my mum, as quickly as possible,' she instructed.

'What? Why?' asked Edie, her face draining of colour as she considered her friend's renewed energy with caution. 'Where are you going?'

'Out there,' Marina declared, looking at the pier which swung ominously on the silent sea.

'*Again*?' the girls cried in unison, causing Thea to drop her thermos which hit the ground with an explosion of warm pumpkin tea.

'I think William will be there. He has to be! But you'll need to get my mum quickly, before anyone else has the chance to figure out where he might be hiding.'

'But, Marina—'

'But nothing! I have to find him and put things right. He has to know the truth before Harold gets his greasy mitts on him and he's locked up for ever, or *worse*.'

'The truth?' asked Thea quizzically, while Edie looked to the ground in awkwardness.

Neither had time to protest further as Marina was already tumbling down the beach to the surf, where a collection of rowing boats lay abandoned at the bottom of the cliff path. Taking up two oars that someone had helpfully left alongside, she pushed one of the boats into the shallow waters before throwing herself inside.

The sea glimmered, as still as a mirror as Marina glided through the low waves like a knife in butter. She saw Edie and Thea begin to fade away as their shapes fled up the beach and along the promenade, back towards the high street where large crowds were spilling from the narrow streets and on to the sand for the evening's bonfire celebrations.

The first time Marina had made this treacherous journey across the turbulent sea, she'd felt foolish, silly and stubborn. Now, a calm and sturdy determination helped propel her boat forward with the greatest sense of purpose. After what seemed like no time at all, she had reached the crippled old pier and was throwing a thin rope, which she had already tied into a perfect Honda knot, around the same nail bashed crudely into the side of the swaying stilts. The line that had snapped on her previous visit still swung limply in the breeze, and she pulled it free before tossing it to the floor of her boat.

Marina scrabbled up the crippled wharf and stepped over the broken door which remained rotting on the floor. She peered into the darkness, her heart in her mouth as the same stench of salt and squid found its way into her nostrils.

'William? Are you here?'

She stumbled blindly about the room, holding her breath for the smell of fish as she searched the soggy floor for a box of matches that she knew had to be there. Finding them at last beneath the cracked window, she struck one and the new light helped her spy William's old stub of a candle at her feet. After igniting the wick, she held it high in the air and scanned the room. Empty, except for William's bed – his lumpy pile of nets and tin cans – as well as the mouldy heap of toys and blankets. A large hermit crab, which seemed to shriek in silent terror as the light revealed its hiding place, scuttled to a corner and collapsed through a ragged hole into the water below.

With a deep sigh Marina placed the candle on the windowsill, just as she had seen it little more than a week ago, on the night this had all begun. William wasn't here, and she had wasted valuable time in which she could have been tracking him down. She was certain there was more to Harold's story . . . If there really had been some kind of run-in, then William would have needed to defend himself and would know to keep a low profile. But what could have forced him to take a pinch at Harold? Marina had always detested the fishmonger, with his continuous attempts to drive her mum out of business, but was he capable of causing William physical harm? Could *Harold* be the one behind the whole story?

Stumped, Marina collapsed heavily on to the bed of nets with a shriek of pain, having landed on something hard and sharp ... After rolling off the pile and massaging her sore bum, she tore back the first few layers of netting, expecting to find a treasure trove of tin cans and other junk. Instead, she discovered an enormous stash of fireworks, rigged and ready to be ignited.

Back on the seafront, the people of Merlington were beginning their Bonfire Night celebrations in earnest, wary of William's new-found status as a dangerous, out-of-control animal but reluctant to let him ruin their festivities. The crowd that surrounded Harold and Sally had dispersed and she could finally talk frankly, having followed him down to the beach.

'Harold, I assure you that there's been some kind of misunderstanding. I don't know what could have caused William to take a snap at you, if that is what happened, but it will all be one big mix-up.'

'If that's so, why'd 'e do a runner, eh?' jabbed Walter, who was still looking to Harold for direction as he stuck to their agreed version of events with aplomb.

'He won't have gone far, don't worry. As soon as I've found him, we'll come down to the beach and this will all be cleared up. I've no doubt Marina has found him already,' she said, realizing as she did that her daughter had not followed the crowd. She turned and walked swiftly back towards the main road, picking up speed as she anxiously disappeared around the corner and out of sight.

'Harold,' urged Walter. 'I'm not so sure about this no more. What the hake are we gonna do if she finds 'im? I'm done for if it gets out that I've been thwackin' people round the head with an oar for no good reason.'

'We've seen the last of him, don't you worry,' boomed Harold. He reached into his coat pocket and pulled out a fresh packet of crabsticks. 'He'd be a fool to show his face here again, now that our story has done its damage. Tonight, once his old shack is sent to the bottom of the sea in a shower of fireworks, there'll be nowhere for him to come home to. He's long gone, mark my words.'

'Are you sure 'bout that?' Walter gasped, as Harold took a huge chomp on a fistful of meat.

Harold looked up to where the landlord was pointing a skeletal finger, and choked on the snack as he focused on the faint light from a small candle, flickering on the windowsill of the shack on the old pier.

CHAPTER THIRTY-TWO

Fireworks

'Marina! Marina, are you here?'

Sally burst through the front door of Minnow's, her eyes darting around the empty store. The only answer she received was the echo of her own voice, followed by silence. Behind the glass counter, the sneeze guards still in desperate need of a wipe, the day's leftover fish was beginning to whiff as it wallowed in a frosty slush like a snowy pile in the roadside gutter.

'Mrs Minnow?'

Sally jumped at the new voice, turning around to be faced only with the store's lumpy tower of knitted William toys. She scanned the pile in confusion, before finally spotting a pale, rubbery face visible from within the heap of wool.

'William! Thank goodness,' she sighed, quickly lowering the window blinds and switching off a handful of the fluorescent lights with trepidation. 'Where have you been?'

As William climbed from his cosy hiding place, the mound of toys in his own image cascading to the floor with a soft bounce, Sally considered her strange ward. She took in his immense, rusty claws which were held timidly together at his waist, his tentacle hair shivering in the cold air and framing his kind, nervous face. She had never seen him look younger. He was only a child, practically the same age as Marina and *far* more wholesome. If there had been any doubt in her mind, Sally was certain now that everything Harold had claimed was a lie.

'It's all right,' she assured him. 'Harold told us you snapped him, but I know you would only have done so in self-defence. Tell me what really happened, and it will all be OK.'

William cringed at the question, mortified to have resorted to violence and deeply ashamed of the embarrassment he must have caused his new family. Sally and Marina had shown him nothing but kindness, and this was how he had repaid them.

'I'm so sorry, Mrs Minnow. I really didn't mean to. They hit me around the head with an oar, and I fell overboard. I floated in the water, dazed for a second or two, and the next thing I knew I was being pulled towards the boat by my claw. I didn't know what they would do with me if they got me back on board.' He flinched. 'I was so scared.'

Sally felt the blood boil in her veins and her ears rang with the angry blast of a thousand shipping horns.

'They did *what*? That awful, evil, horrible coward! How could he be so despicable? And what on earth was he trying to do?'

William pulled a stool from behind the counter and motioned for Sally to sit, which she did with a very deep breath, in and out, to compose herself.

'Why did you go with them?' she asked. 'What

could they have said to make you think it was safe to go out to *sea*? I thought you were just collecting seaweed and having a look in the harbour for the che—' Her tummy lurched. She knew now that there was no longer anything to be found at the bottom of the sea outside Merlington, Marina having pulled the crumbling chest and its secrets from the depths more than a week ago.

'Harold said something about my father.' He blushed and his translucent grey cheeks clouded over. 'I thought he might know something that could help me find him.'

'Your father?' Sally spluttered. 'What would he think he knew about that?' Her stomach flipped frantically again at the knowledge she possessed and continued to keep from William with every word she uttered.

'William,' she started with a considered pause as she contemplated the best way to break the news. 'The man you know as your father—'

Thea Marigold unexpectedly burst through the door with a *thump*, startling Sally and sending William tumbling backwards into a pile of crates that crashed to the floor of the storeroom. Edie Krill followed closely behind, skidding to a halt on the slippery tiles.

'Thea, Edie, what's going on?'

'Mrs Minnow, you have to . . . William! You're here!' Thea's eyes widened at the sight of William before she was overcome with shyness at having addressed him so directly.

'Girls, what's the matter? Have you seen Marina?'

'Yes, that's exactly why we've come!' scowled Edie, knocking Thea in the side with her elbow. 'She's rowing over to the old pier, she's probably there right now.'

'What? Why?'

'Because, well . . .' Thea turned to William again with sudden confidence, as the strange boy picked himself up from the floor with a shake of his tentacles. 'She thought *you* would be there.'

Sally grabbed her keys from the counter and scooped Edie, Thea and William towards the front door. Then a huge bang erupted in the distance.

'What was that?' she exclaimed in alarm, tearing from the store and out into the night. The street was empty, with all sixteen other fishmongers in town having long closed for the bonfire celebrations. Sally thought she must have imagined the boom, before a long whistle overhead sent her eyes to the sky just in time to see an enormous firework explode in the darkness over the seafront.

'The fireworks have started early,' she realized with relief.

'The pier!' cried Edie, as Sally, Thea and William turned towards the beach to spy the battered old bait shop in the distance. It was too far away usually, to see through the evening gloom, but now it was floodlit by fireworks which flew in rapid succession – straight from the shattered window.

'Marina!' gasped Sally.

Suddenly they were running, down the high street, past The Laughing Trout and out on to the seafront, weaving between the bonfire crowd who oohed and aahed as rockets exploded in the sky with a cascade of colour.

'Sally, over here!'

She turned to see Caroline Carp, frantically pushing her way towards her.

'Sally, Marina is out there!'

'I know,' she assured her, with outstretched arms. 'We're going to get some help, don't panic yet.'

'No, you don't understand. I saw Harold—'

'Harold?'

'Yes,' Caroline pleaded as her eyes widened with urgency. 'He took his boat out to the pier just before the fireworks started. He's there right *now*!'

Without a second's pause, William tore from the group and ran down the beach, ignoring the calls from his friends and the gasps from the crowd as they recognized him. Mrs Cuttle screamed in terror when a tentacle tickled her splayed elbow as he sped by.

'I knew he was a dodgy sort,' she shrieked to anyone in earshot, before noticing the knitted William doll peering from her front coat pocket and quickly stuffing it into the depths.

Reaching the surf, William sprang from his heels and into the sky, before shooting down through the water like one of the bottle rockets firing from his old home. He moved through the icy sea with all the skill of the most decorated Olympic swimmer or the hungriest great white shark, rolling through currents and shoals of curious fish without the slightest hesitation.

As he approached the legs of the old pier, sliding among the silt and sand that barely secured it in place, he looked up to see the shadow of not one, but two boats silhouetted against the dark sky. Picturing Marina's face, he thrust his legs in a flurry of action towards the surface before blasting from the water like a flying fish. He landed gracefully on the edge of the rotting pier and turned to face the darkness of the empty door frame.

CHAPTER THIRTY-THREE

Family Reunion

A flashing Roman candle whizzed angrily towards William's face. He ducked just in time, allowing the firework to zoom over his head, although not before it singed a particularly bouncy tentacle and blasted into the night, spitting red sparks all the way.

'William, it's a trap!' Marina screamed from somewhere in the darkness. 'He kept me here, waiting for you. You're the one he's after!'

Harold jumped from the corner of the shack and smacked William across the head, sending him flying into a heap on the floor. The room was dark except for the colourful blasts of different fireworks which ignited sporadically, illuminating the walls in blues, greens and reds. Marina crawled across the wooden boards and managed to quickly find her friend, despite their blindness.

'This is not how this was supposed to go,' Harold yelled in a frenzy. 'I told you *never* to come back to Merlington, and when I saw that candle you were meant to be out here on your own. I had no idea that *she* was inside when I lit the fuse!'

William rubbed his aching tentacle scalp as he picked himself and Marina up off the floor. They backed into a corner, fireworks continuing to explode dangerously at their side while Harold's face was momentarily brightened by a flash of gold. His wild eyes were visible, fixed on William with a frightening focus as they burnt yellow in the blaze.

'This was supposed to be the greatest bonfire in the history of Merlington, and the perfect way to finally be rid of this eyesore of a pier! But you came back, yet again.' Harold's greasy hair was plastered madly to his forehead, lank and lifeless. 'If the pier goes down with you both inside, then so be it.'

William and Marina looked up through the green haze of a spluttering firecracker, dumbfounded by the deranged man whose beastly silhouette loomed over them from the doorway, still blocking their escape.

'Why?' stuttered Marina, shaking her head in confusion. 'Why do you hate William so much? What has he ever done to you that could have been so terrible?'

'He ruined my life!' bellowed Harold. He struck a match before lighting an oil lamp which finally illuminated his face, the many folds of skin now stretched into an insane sneer of torment. 'He ruined my perfectly normal life with his horrible existence. "You'll turn into a fish one day," they all warned me. My mother practically *promised* me! Well, she was wrong. But just *look* at the son the fates thought acceptable to send my way.'

Marina's jaw hit the floor. 'I knew you had to be involved somehow. You're the one who threw William into the sea . . . *You're* his father!'

'Father?' Harold jeered, lifting the lamp high in one hand and holding the oar out like a sword with the other as he batted a blue bottle rocket through the window. 'If you mean that I'm the one to thank for afflicting Merlington with this monstrosity then, yes, in that sense you could call me his *father*.'

William's tentacles reared up on their ends as what little colour remained in his ghostly skin drained away to complete transparency. 'Tell me everything,' he croaked.

'Don't listen, William,' Marina sniffed as she held him close at her side.

'We tried for so long to have a baby,' Harold choked. 'I was desperate . . . For a child to mould, and to train in the ways of the Reverential Federation of Fishmongers. Someone I could trust to leave in charge of my brilliant legacy!

'I hurled my anger at the sea, the ocean, the universe! Anyone who could possibly be listening. Then one night – one awful night – someone did listen. And they sent us their answer.' He motioned to William with the oar, his top lip curling backwards in disgust.

'But how is that possible?' asked William, shrinking against the wall as Harold's wildness increased with each line of his confession.

'You came to Merlington thirteen years ago, delivered in a box of squid like some cruel joke driven from the depths of the English Channel. When I held you in my arms for the first time and looked down at the monster made to mock me, my mother's words echoed inside my skull. I was appalled, but I knew that you had been sent to us for a reason. There had been no mistake; you were *our* son, all right. A child in my own image. It was Caroline I felt devastated for. She would have been a brilliant mother, but not like this. Not with *that*!'

'Caroline Carp?' gasped Marina, hooked on every word as William's world came crashing down around them. 'She was involved in this?'

'At first she tried to convince me you were a *gift*,' he spat, staring at William. 'We tried to make the best of it, cod knows we tried. You were a baby all alone and so we took you in for a brief moment of insanity, but how could we have ever raised such a thing? I'd have been the laughing stock of Merlington if it was known that *you* were my legacy. A great, giant, flipping fish freak running the Mullet Over after I'm gone? I don't think so!'

'So you threw a defenceless baby into the sea?'

Marina was shaking, fear pumping through each of her limbs. 'William *was* a gift...'

'He was a *curse*!' Harold boomed, as yet another Roman candle skimmed past his face with a purple hiss.

'All he needed was someone to love him,' cried Marina, clinging tightly to William. He held a threatening claw in Harold's direction, which seemed to snap involuntarily as though sensing the danger they faced. 'He needed protection and you abandoned him!'

'How could you blame me? We didn't even name the thing, so ashamed we were once Caroline finally saw sense. She came round to the suggestion that I row out and dump the baby back where it came from. It ruined us, though, the guilt and regret festering inside of her. She blames me for everything to this day, of course. Hanging around outside Minnow's like an injured puppy, trying to catch a glimpse of him.'

An especially angry Catherine wheel sprang from the floor and hit the wall beside William, showering the room in yellow sparks as it spun out of control. Marina instinctively threw her arms above her head and slammed her face to the ground, feeling as she did so a crack where the floorboard appeared to be weak.

'And it was you,' she continued to press Harold as she looked up through her fingers, the firework having finally fizzled out with a wheeze. 'You dumped that chest in the harbour, the night I first met William.'

Harold sighed in exhaustion as his story continued to unravel. 'A chest of clothes and toys that Caroline had bought in the days when a *normal* baby had not been out of the question. It was the only thing left after she'd finally walked out, so I kept it as a memento of her. Then I hear you and that insufferable Krill girl, jabbering away outside my shop about a wonderful boy with crab claws for hands. I didn't want to believe that you had actually discovered him, but I had to get rid of the chest to be safe. People had known we were an item, of course, but not that we'd tried for a child and certainly not that we'd been saddled with such an abomination. I couldn't risk anyone linking us to it.'

Marina had stood to join William, tapping the weak floorboard with the heel of her foot. She felt it begin to give way while Harold, distracted by his own confession, regurgitated his story like one of the mangy seagulls that followed him around.

'How can any of this be possible?' William asked in disbelief. 'How can you be my father?'

'He isn't, William,' urged Marina, suddenly diverted from her plan.

'But he—'

'Harold abandoned you! He betrayed you! You're kind and sweet and brave. Anyone with half a brain could've seen that you were a gift, sent to our town by the sea for a reason. You saved my life; you could *never* be a curse!' Marina's voice cracked with emotion. 'Some people get to choose their family, and it was the *fisherman* who chose you. He was the one who saved you, and took on the responsibility that Harold and Caroline selfishly refused. Your father is the one who built a home for you, hung pictures on the wall of your shack and looked after you for so many years. The man who loved you enough to make that sacrifice!'

With a deep sigh of resolve she reached into her pocket, and to William's surprise, pulled forth the small photo of Nigel Minnow, who smiled up at them with his toothy grin.

CHAPTER THIRTY-FOUR

The Fisherman

'My gosh, that's him! Marina, you found him!'
Beneath his chest of scales William's heart pounded with adrenaline. Excitement rippled through each of his tentacles like an electric current, as he finally laid eyes on the man he'd been missing for so long. In that moment, the long days and longer months spent waiting on this same pier all seemed worthwhile.

'How did you get this photo? How did you find him?'

'This is my dad too, William. This is Nigel Minnow.' Marina put the picture in her coat, before cradling William's amber claw between both her palms. 'He was the fisherman we've wanted to find for all this time, all along. Our dad.'

William looked into her eyes, overcome with delight and jubilation. Then he furrowed his brow, as one thought floated to the surface of his mind like a giant, angry bubble rising from the depths. He realized what all of this meant, and what Marina was leading up to.

'He's gone, William ... He's lost.'

'But you said he might come back?' he urged, channelling Marina's recently forgotten optimism. 'Maybe he *was* saved by a bale of sea turtles, and now it's amnesia that keeps him from finding his way back. One day he'll appear on the horizon, in his old fishing boat, and return to us for good.'

A maniacal laugh rumbled against the wooden boards of the swaying shack, which seemed to suddenly close inwards as Marina and William were reminded of Harold's intimidating presence. His great figure bore down on them, doubled over in hysterics.

'I'm sorry, William,' Marina croaked. 'I'm not sure that he will be coming back.'

'He won't,' interrupted Harold. His broad smile was lit a wicked shade of crimson by a firework, which ricocheted off the wall behind him in a flurry of cinders. 'I made sure of that six years ago when I gave him a good whack around the head with my oar and watched as he fell beneath the crushing waves. I waited until I was sure he wasn't coming back up.'

Marina's eyes filled with tears of rage. She ran at him with her fists outstretched but was held back by William, whose arm was clamped around her waist.

'You monster! How *could* you?' she cried. 'I knew you had something to do with all this. You took my dad from me when I was only six years old! Was throwing a baby into the sea not enough?'

'I did what I had to, as I always have. Your father left me with no choice once I heard him down The Laughing Trout with his batty mum one night, drunkenly telling her about the baby he'd seen being tossed in the sea! How he'd rescued the child, nurtured it in secret, and hoped to move the boy into the family home.'

Marina's heart panged at the thought, her tears stinging as they turned from anger to sadness. She wilted in William's hold and he fell backwards, listening to the words which spewed from Harold like steam.

'I knew exactly what he was talking about, of course, though anyone else would have thought him a rambling drunk. He'd spotted a bundle being chucked overboard and curiosity got the better of him, no doubt! Probably thought that he was pulling in some treasure when he hauled his fishing net up from the depths. I couldn't be sure whether he'd seen it was me through the darkness, but I took action . . . Your father seemed to think the danger had passed, but I was still on my guard – even after all of these years. Not that it helped me find out where Nigel hid the wretched creature.'

'I don't believe it,' Marina whispered, clamping her eyes shut as the few remaining fireworks were finally snuffed out at her side. She hugged William as they mourned the years they might have spent together, as well as the father they'd both have known.

'This has probably worked out for the best after all,' jeered Harold, backing towards the empty doorway. 'I have you to thank for that, Marina. Now I can be sure that no one will ever know the truth of where he came from.'

Harold lifted his lamp high in the air before slamming it to the floor between them, smashing it to pieces with a roar of fire. The oil quickly spilt across the damp beams, ablaze and wild as it stretched the width of the room and leapt up the dry, cracked walls in an eruption of orange heat. The crusty, mould-covered painting of sailing boats swiftly melted to goo in its charred frame.

'William!' screamed Marina, over the thunderous crackle of burning wood. 'On the count of three, we need to jump together. Do you understand?'

He nodded as she took his arm under hers, sweat running down both of their faces as the flames licked the ceiling and Marina once again found the small crack in the floor. She began to count.

'One . . . two . . . three . . . now!'

They jumped in unison, landing together on the weakened floorboard, which broke immediately on impact. They fell straight through, hurtling towards the water below and causing the shack to crumble inwards as the unstable beams gave way with a moan. Harold ran for his boat as timbers and planks flew in every direction. The swaying stilts that held the building aloft lost control as they waved violently, snapping in two, before the entire pier crumbled into the sea with a shower of splinters.

Marina was already swaddled in darkness by the time she felt the icy sting of the autumn water, sharp on her skin. Beneath the sea she twisted and turned, not sure which way was up or down, barely aware of the enormous chunks of wood and plank that fell past her through the gloom before sinking towards the depths.

She swam in her blindness, struggling to move forward as her lungs screamed for oxygen. She stretched her arms upwards, the tips of her fingers searching desperately for the surface but only finding the cold sand of the dusty sea floor. Horrified, she spun in circles fuelled by confusion and fear, her head dizzy and her legs growing weaker. The blurry, black shapes that swirled around her began to slow, fading into nothingness as her senses flickered and failed . . .

Then, a large, hard claw was in her hand. She clung to it with the last of her strength, as it pulled her through the shadows and up towards the surface. She broke free into the bright starry night with an enormous cough and a salty splutter, and just as quickly the tentacle boy at her side was gone.

'Marina!'

Her mother was there, in the bow of a speedboat beside her friends, shining a torch in Marina's face as Edie and Peter Featherfin each put an arm under hers and hauled her on board with a splash.

'Marina, thank cod! We just saw the pier collapse and I feared the worst. I can't tell you how scared I was! My darling,' Sally gushed. Her arms were wrapped around Marina in a bear hug as she showered her sopping daughter with kisses.

'Mum, where's William?'

'He was with you?' asked Thea. 'He managed to get to you in time?'

'He was here!' Marina cried, searching the waves with her bloodshot eyes. 'He was just here, right now! He pulled me up from underwater when I couldn't find my way.'

'We haven't seen him,' said Edie, wringing her wet hair over the side of the boat. 'You just appeared on the surface, suddenly right next to us.'

'It's true,' said Peter, scratching his head. 'You just . . . turned up!'

'But he was right *there*! He saved me – *again*!'

'William can handle himself in the water,' Sally urged. 'We need to get you back to land and dry you off, as quickly as possible.'

Wrapped in a blanket and munching on a bar of chocolate that Peter had pulled from the sleeve of his duffle coat, Marina recounted everything she'd heard. From the strange delivery of the box of baby squid, to the mysterious trunk of clothes and toys, and the real reason behind her father's disappearance. As Sally listened to the tale of her husband's final encounter with Harold, she dug her chipped nails into the side of the speedboat with grief. She had always known the fishmonger to be a nasty piece of work, more so than anyone else was willing to believe, but this? It broke her heart to imagine Nigel, alone in the water, and all for remaining the kind and caring man that she had felt lucky to marry. She longed to see him one last time, to tell him how proud she was . . .

'What happened to Harold?' Sally asked her daughter finally, summoning up the greatest self-composure she could muster.

'After William and I jumped through the floor the whole place came crashing down. Harold won't have had any time to get back to a boat.'

'He'll have drowned!' cried Thea.

'That's if he wasn't crushed by falling beams first,' mused Peter thoughtfully.

'Good riddance,' slammed Edie.

Marina pulled her blanket tighter. 'No,' she whispered as the others turned to her with surprise. 'He has to pay! If he's survived the fall and the freezing water, we have to make sure the police are waiting when he washes up on the shore.'

Sally smiled at her daughter, impressed by her maturity and proud of her resolve. 'Then let's make sure we're there first,' she said, pulling on the boat's motor and speeding towards the crowds on the beach.

CHAPTER THIRTY-FIVE

The Horizon

*H*arold awoke, face down on the wet sand, barely conscious of the foamy waves lapping at his earlobes or the gaggle of seagulls nesting on the back of his head, cawing with excitement at their overgrown catch. He slowly began to roll over, sending the hungry gulls flying except for one unlucky bird which found itself squashed beneath him as his enormous body flopped over like a beached whale.

'What the hake—'

Harold's head began to pound as a large bump on his forehead pulsated. After a falling beam inside the shack had whacked him across the temple, he'd swum towards the shore before losing consciousness. The gulls, settled again beside his swollen scalp, were now happily pecking away with their sharp beaks.

'My head!' he cried, batting away the birds and covering his face with his hands, accidentally rubbing sand into his eyes and groaning in agony from the sting.

'Mr Mole?'

Harold's bleary eyes snapped open painfully to find two men standing over him, their silhouettes unfamiliar in the moonlight.

'Mr Mole, can you hear me?'

His cloudy vision adjusted and the figures gradually became clear. They were policemen, each one wearing a fluorescent yellow jacket and a black peaked cap, emblazoned with a shiny silver badge. Harold sat bolt upright, his head hammering as the squashed bird was released from beneath him and finally able to limp away in a zigzag of confusion.

'Evening, officers,' said Harold with a betraying

wobble. 'Quite a to-do out there, that pier was dangerous! Should've been knocked down years ago, if you ask me. A complete eyesore.'

'We've heard all about what happened on the pier,' said the younger of the two officers, helping Harold to his feet. 'I'm afraid we're going to need you to come down to the station with us.'

The remaining bonfire crowds, clutching cups of mulled wine or coffee, had begun to gather round, and now lined the seafront with interest.

'Come . . . come down to the station? There won't be any need for that,' said Harold, puffing out his chest. 'It's that tentacle-haired fish freak you need to speak with. He attacked me! Clawed up my shoulder and left me to bleed out!'

Harold pulled down his collar, the dramatic effect of the small wound now entirely removed thanks to his soaking wet shirt which was clean of blood.

'Your associate has already told us the whole story, Mr Mole.'

The second, taller officer motioned towards the flashing blue lights of a police car parked on the promenade. Inside, Walter Whitby sat on the back seat and pressed his sorry face against the glass window. Harold felt the air closing around him.

'Well, he's the one who belted the monster 'round the head, not me!' He grabbed his mouth in horror as he heard the words tumbling out.

'We're more interested in your attempt to burn down the old pier while two children were inside,' said the young policeman.

Harold began to grow flustered, his head swimming with panic and his skin growing clammy and warm.

'There's really an explanation for all of this, I assure you,' he pleaded.

'You can tell us all about it at the station.'

The two officers led Harold up the beach towards the flashing blue lights of their car as shells crunched beneath his soggy shoes. They moved slowly through the gawping crowds, the people of Merlington pointing and whispering as Harold scanned their disapproving faces for help.

'I'm innocent!' he roared, struggling to dig his feet into the sand. 'Everything I did, I did for Merlington! To keep you people safe! TO MAINTAIN SOME NORMALITY!'

Reaching their car, the taller policeman opened

the door and pushed Harold inside, forcing Walter to quickly slide across the back seat so as not to be squashed under the fishmonger's mighty weight.

'Officers,' said a voice. The men turned to face Caroline Carp, who stood resolutely by the car. 'I think you'll want to speak with me too.'

'Were you out on the pier as well, miss?' asked the younger policeman in confusion.

'No,' Caroline whispered. 'But if you listen to what I have to say, then you'll see I'm as responsible for all of this as Harold.'

The officers exchanged a look of uncertainty, before shrugging and helping Caroline climb inside the back of the car next to a crushed Walter. As they set their siren and began to drive along the promenade, Harold continued to shout and protest until his voice was no longer audible to the crowds on the beach. The car rounded the corner of the high street and disappeared from sight.

Marina and Sally had watched it all, sitting on the steps outside a boarded-up beach hut and huddled under Marina's thick, woollen blanket.

'Is that it, then?' asked Marina through her tiredness. 'Is it over?'

'Well,' started Sally. 'There will likely be a trial, and we may need to tell our story once again in court . . . But I can safely say Harold won't be coming back here for a very long time.'

'And what about Caroline?'

'Perhaps she'll find some peace at last,' Sally said reflectively. 'She was obviously keen to atone in some way, for how she treated William all those years ago.'

Marina laid her head on her mother's shoulder with a heavy sigh, exhaustion washing over her like the evening tide.

'Sally? Marina?'

They looked up to find themselves met by the faces of Merlington's many fishmongers, each one painted with the same expression of discomfort.

'We're so sorry,' said Cheryl Shoal, her voice cracking with regret. 'We had no idea that Harold would ever go that far . . .'

'We got caught up in the madness,' sniffed Deirdre Bream, blowing her nose into a crusty old hand-kerchief. 'Burnin' down the pier with two young 'uns inside, it's just awful.'

'We knew that he was desperate to be rid of William,' Alan Thropp started. 'But—'

'We thought he was just a fish!' finished Ian, the twin brothers bowing their heads in a united display of shame. Marina and her mother listened in silence; their hands entwined in a comforting, pincer-like hold.

'I'm not sure that any of us actually took Harold serious,' croaked Shrimpy. 'We just . . . We wanted things to get back to normal. We wanted to see some customers again!'

'And now we all know how you must've felt, before all this happened,' sobbed Deirdre.

Cheryl clicked her turquoise fingernails together awkwardly. 'We couldn't see past the tentacles or the scales. We couldn't see William for the boy he is. We can now, and we want you to know that.'

After a moment, Sally nodded firmly. 'He's family.'

Several minutes later, having expressed their sorrow and remorse one by one, the fishmongers slowly drifted away along the promenade and the Minnows were alone once more. Marina looked into her mother's eyes as her own began to grow wet.

'I'm sorry for getting us into this, Mum.'

Sally straightened up and took her daughter's face gently in both hands.

'My darling,' she tutted. 'You have nothing to be sorry for. You were absolutely brilliant. If it wasn't for your imaginative and inquisitive mind, Harold would still be running this town. We'd have never known the truth about your father. We'd have never met William!'

They hugged tightly, tears running down Marina's rosy right cheek.

'Come on,' said Sally. 'We need to get you home and to bed. It's been a very long day.'

'We can't,' urged Marina. 'We can't leave while he's still out there!'

She looked out to sea, scanning the white horses which galloped across the surface, praying to see a flick of a tentacle or the shimmer of scales among the cresting manes in the moonlight.

'He knows where we are,' Sally spoke softly. 'He knows exactly where to find us and that he will always be welcome, whenever he might feel ready to come home.'

Marina returned her head to her mother's shoulder, as if to confirm the decision that they would be waiting a while longer.

'If only Dad had been able to tell us,' Marina said,

breaking the silence after a moment. 'We could have been a real family for William.'

Sally stroked her daughter's long brown hair as she imagined how different their lives might have been.

'He thought it was too dangerous,' she said, after a contemplative pause. 'He was right to be cautious, not knowing who it was that had abandoned William nor how far they'd go to keep their secret. He had to make sure that William was safe.'

Marina listened to the waves, which softly lapped at the shore over the low buzz of the crowds left milling around the promenade. Her eyes were still fixed on the horizon.

'Do you think he'll ever come back?'

'William can look after himself, don't you worry.'

'Not William,' Marina said. 'Dad.'

Sally took another long pause, eventually kissing her daughter softly on the scalp.

'I don't know, sweetheart.'

'But we can still hope?' asked Marina, looking up into her mother's hazel eyes.

'We can,' Sally smiled. 'We can most certainly hope. Perhaps he got caught in the net of a huge French fishing trawler, and he's working off the debt at a cafe in Calais.'

Marina smiled softly at her mother's story.

'And one day,' Sally continued, 'when we least expect it, he will appear on the horizon—'

'In his old fishing boat!' interrupted Marina.

'In his old fishing boat,' beamed Sally. 'And he'll come back to us for good.'

They sat like that for another half an hour, warm beneath their blanket and staring out to sea as the bonfire crowds slowly dispersed. Once the street-lights began to dim and the only sound left was the push and pull of the waves, Marina stood to follow her mother the short distance home.

Then, with one final parting glance to the horizon, they saw it. There in the starlight, so quickly it could easily have been missed, an iridescent body of scales sliding gracefully over the water, away from land and into the distance. A marvellous head of tentacles flapping in the breeze, as if waving goodbye.

Storyteller

High above the sleepy town of Merlington, perched on the edge of a craggy bluff, the walls of Granny Minnow's care home whistled as the December wind howled through gaps in the stone. Far below, the churning sea at high tide had eaten another half an inch from the cliff walls, which kept the eerie building upright and looming large over the seafront.

It was Christmas Day, which meant the care home was quieter than usual, operating on a skeleton staff and with many of the residents visiting their friends and families. The entrance hall was decorated with metallic foil garlands that streamed across the ceiling, while thick strips of fluffy tinsel in golds, greens and reds glistened on the reception desk and snaked around the staircase banister. On the large, wooden front door hung an enormous wreath made of shells in the shape of a starfish, which was slowly being pecked apart by hungry gulls.

Marina sat with her mother and grandmother in the communal lounge, curled up in a cosy ball of fullness following their baked sea bass lunch with all the trimmings. Each of them wore a sparkly paper hat, while Sally played sleepily with a plastic thimble and Granny Minnow continued to laugh at her cracker joke: *Why did the lobster blush? Because the sea weed.*

As the Queen appeared on the television for her annual address, Marina was ushered towards the set to turn up the volume. Having no interest in watching, she left the warmth of the sitting room and wandered over to the patio doors, beyond which lay a beautifully manicured garden. It was lined by flower beds that hibernated beneath a light blanket of frost, and hedgerows carved into spirals of green. A coil of twinkling fairy lights weaved itself tightly through the vegetation.

Marina folded herself into a pretzel on the springy, cushioned window seat and pressed her face against the glass with a yawn. She had barely been able to concentrate on anything for weeks, faking enthusiasm for the humdrum of daily life as unconvincingly as she had faked her enthusiasm for Christmas. The only thing to have raised a smile on her face was the gold locket now hanging around her neck, which she had opened under the Christmas tree to reveal two portraits inside – the same photo of her father she'd torn from the family album, and one of William clipped from the local newspaper. She puffed her cheeks and let out a long, heavy breath that fogged the window with condensation, watching as a drip of water ran down the glass and cut through her vision.

Suddenly behind the translucent fog of her own making was a blur of movement. Marina wiped the window with the cuff of her jumper to see a man walking through the grounds with a young girl on his arm. As she helped her grandfather navigate the slippery stone courtyard, the girl's birdlike features were more pronounced than usual due to her brown duffle coat which she held close to her body, her bright red jumper pulled up to her nose like the breast of a robin. Wendy caught sight of Marina on her seat in the window as she helped her grandfather up the step to his garden room, before gently lowering him into a large wing-backed armchair that looked particularly squishy. She kissed him gently on the cheek before once again entering the frosty garden and crossing the courtyard towards the patio doors.

Marina sat up with a defensive energy as Wendy came inside from the cold and stood before her sheepishly, her face still buried in the wool of her jumper.

'Merry Christmas, Marina,' she stuttered. 'I hope you've had a nice day.'

Marina surveyed her with a look that was half suspicion, half disbelief.

'Thanks,' she said with caution, perched on the edge of her seat and ready to pounce at a moment's notice. 'What are you doing here?'

'Visiting my grandad. My mum dropped me off

after lunch to spend some time with him while she goes to see—' She paused, looking awkwardly down to her fur-lined caramel boots. 'To see my dad.'

Marina watched as Wendy's cheeks turned pink and felt her own stomach lurch in a surprising show of sympathy.

'Sit down, if you'd like,' she offered, unfurling her legs and shimmying her bum along the window seat while pretending not to notice the embarrassment.

'Thanks,' chirped Wendy, taking up the newly vacated spot and sitting clumsily on top of her hands. She swung her legs with unease. They'd barely made eye contact in weeks. 'Marina, I'm sorry.'

Marina spluttered in amazement. 'You are?'

'Yes. For everything my dad and Harold said. I'm sorry for believing them.'

'It was Harold, mainly,' Marina conceded generously.

'Yeah.' Wendy bit the collar of her jumper. 'My dad helped, though. Even if he didn't understand the whole story, he helped cover up Harold's lies.'

'Well,' smiled Marina. 'We both know how much you hate liars.'

Wendy flushed pink once again, but this time she held Marina's gaze. Finally, she smiled, and the two girls giggled with only a hint of unease.

'I'm sorry for that most of all,' said Wendy with genuine warmth. 'You aren't a liar, really. I get it now. You're a storyteller.'

Now it was Marina's turn to blush. 'Do you really think there's a difference?'

'Lies cause people hurt,' scowled Wendy. 'Whether you want them to or not. Your stories make people laugh. I was just jealous, of your imagination. Your ability to make up your own happy endings when you need to.'

Marina smiled. 'Thank you. I'm sorry too. I definitely know the best ways to wind you up,' she cringed.

Wendy laughed and continued to swing her legs. 'Will you tell me a story?'

'What, now? Why?' asked Marina, buoyed by the request from her former detractor. 'I haven't really felt like telling stories in the last few weeks.'

'Well, it's Christmas. And I think we could both do with a bit of cheering up,' said Wendy with a knowing smile.

'OK,' Marina laughed. 'I'll try . . .'

Her eyes darted around the sitting room but found

little inspiration among the chintz cushions, garish decorations and stuffy lace curtains. Scratching the back of her head in thought, Marina's thumb caught the chain still hanging from her neck as she looked down at the golden locket resting on her chest . . .

CHAPTER THIRTY-SEVEN

Marina's Story

'There was once a fisherman.' Marina smiled as she saw the story forming in her mind like a daydream – a feeling she'd sorely missed. 'The kindest, most caring fisherman anyone had ever known. He loved his family more than anything, but one tragic winter's night he was taken from them. Smacked across the head by an oar, for protecting the people he loved, he fell beneath the waves and was lost to the sea.

'But he lived, floating through the open water for what seemed like days, rolling in and out of consciousness as he bobbed on the waves, dipping under the surface just long enough to snap out of his slumber and continue treading water in an effort to stay afloat.

'Eventually, through bleary eyes and salt-encrusted eyelashes, he spied land. A curious, grey, fleshy island that seemed to bob in the water. He climbed the bulbous mound with the last of his energy, reaching the crest with a heave and a groan before collapsing in relief. He wasn't afforded the time to rest for long, though, as in a moment of terror the fisherman realized the island was beginning to move – not just up and down, but through the water with a sudden lurch of speed and power. As the island sank sharply beneath the waves, and as he continued to cling to the only surface he had purchase on, looking through the crystal waters of the Atlantic he learnt that he was hanging on to the back of an enormous humpback whale – which was now dragging him deeper and deeper into open ocean.

'The fisherman held his breath for as long as he could, for what seemed like an eternity, until with a gasp and a groan his lungs were finally filled with crisp, cold oxygen. In his delight and relief, it was a few seconds before he recognized the strange reality that he was still clinging to the whale's enormous pectoral fins despite no longer being in the water. He looked to the sky in horror to meet the faces of a crew of baying sailors, staring down at him and their colossal catch. He was trapped in the tangled net of an illegal whaling boat, the humpback now being pulled hungrily towards the deck. Running on nothing but adrenaline and instinct, the fisherman climbed through a gap between the gargantuan ropes, scrabbling up the side of the net to the hook which held them both aloft. Ignoring the furious cries of the whalers, he pulled back a lever on the enormous winch. As the net flew open he watched the whale fall, with a heavy splash, back into the depths.

'Well, of course, the crew were spoiling for a fight, deprived of their enormous catch and the glory that would await them upon returning to land with barrels full of blubber and oil. But their anger was extinguished almost immediately. After hauling the fisherman on board it became obvious that the poor soul had lost his memory to the waves – his mind apparently deprived of oxygen for just a moment too long.

'What he hadn't lost was his strong sense of right and wrong, nor his warm affinity for the sea and all its inhabitants. With no home or family that he could remember, the fisherman stayed on board the whaling ship and decided to teach the crew a kinder way to make a living. Rather than robbing the ocean of its most extraordinary creatures, under the fisherman's guidance the sailors turned their back on hunting to form an ocean patrol team and an international charity. With the fisherman installed as their head advisor, they navigated the Atlantic, rescuing creatures great and small from the tangled nets and sharp harpoons of poachers.

'It was after many years of sailing the seas that one cold December evening the ship cruised across the English Channel and stumbled upon a small boat which spewed thick, black clouds of smoke. And there, hanging from the boat's rusty fishing hook, was a friend from what felt like another life entirely. A boy, now a teenager, his body covered in iridescent scales that twinkled in the setting sun. No hands but gigantic, amber claws that tried their best to release a thick, glistening tentacle from the hook above as he swung in the air from his rubbery scalp. It was his son!

'Everything came back to him in an instant, memories flooding his mind like a burst drainpipe in a basement flat. Not only was this the boy the fisherman had raised by himself in secret, but the family that would be waiting for him at home were now at the forefront of his thoughts. He leapt to action, unhooking his scaly son from the line as the sailors aboard both boats looked on in amazement at this most peculiar of scenes.

'After an evening of hugs, and a sumptuous supper of salmon en croûte in celebration of their unexpected reunion, the fisherman and his son bid their friends goodbye and were gifted a small motorboat to make their long journey home. And so they sped off into the night and towards the south coast of Britain, to their family, who they knew would be waiting for them with open hearts and open arms.'

Marina finished her story, pulling her legs up on to the chair and hugging her knees close. The girls sat in silent contemplation for a few short moments.

'Thanks, Marina,' Wendy smiled softly as she rose from the window seat and tightly buttoned the toggles on her coat. 'It looks like you've got your gift for storytelling back.'

'Merry Christmas, Wendy,' Marina beamed. She bid her new friend goodbye, watching thoughtfully as she crossed the garden patio to join her grandfather in the warmth.

After a moment, Marina rose too and walked towards the sitting room and her family. She found Granny Minnow fast asleep in her armchair, happily humming along to the television in her dreams as it blasted an old family musical that Marina was sure played every single Christmas. Sally, meanwhile, was reading on the sofa, devouring the Japanese cookbook which her daughter had found for a gift.

Marina turned to the windowsill and collapsed on her arms with a sigh. Looking out to sea, she wondered where William could be right now. What would have taken him away from them, without so much as a proper goodbye? She hadn't even been given the chance to thank him for saving her life – twice.

And then, just as suddenly as she had started to think of her friend, some movement on the sea caught Marina's eye.

Could it be . . . ?

She squinted into the December sun, praying that her instincts were right as a shadowy shape on the water grew larger and clearer with every wave that broke on the shore . . .

It is!

Screaming with excitement, she grabbed her mother's arm and scooped her up and out of the room, the cookbook thumping from her hands. As they tore through the front door and out into the crisp winter air, gulls went flying and the shell wreath fell to the ground with a clatter.

Granny Minnow smacked her lips as she woke up to realize the lounge had emptied. Tutting, she pulled herself up from her comfy, fraying armchair and walked over to the window slowly. Throwing her head back as her eyelids flapped free of mascara, she looked down to see Marina and Sally bowling down the cliff path towards the beach.

There in the shallows, a small fishing boat was coming in to land, carrying two figures who hopped majestically from the vessel and into the surf. The man she recognized from another lifetime, his kind, smiling face weathered by age and his thinning, frizzy hair a white to match hers. The boy she did not know, but he had the most fantastic head of tentacles.

EPILOGUE

Six Months Later

*T*he warm yellow sand of Merlington's beach was littered with bodies, white, red and brown, as people flocked from towns close by to lie spread-eagled on multicoloured towels. They lined the shore, like long rows of trout baking in the heat, their splayed limbs glistening in the early summer sun. Children splashed in the still-chilly water, kicking up foam and leaping from inflatable dolphins while beads of sweat ran through white slabs of sun cream, mixing together in a lumpy sheen of mottled grease on their backs. Meanwhile, lengthy queues of men and women covered the promenade, where Sole Brothers were back to selling trays of succulent scallops and Minnow's new takeaway cart offered ice-cold platters of fresh sashimi. The seafront would always have been a little busy by late June, but this was ridiculous!

The peculiar boy with crab claws for hands slept soundly on the sand, his translucent skin cooking gently under the warmth of the midday sun. A handful of seagulls, which had gathered in a curious heap by his legs, readied themselves to take a bite of the wriggling toes that fanned a tasty fragrance across the beach. Marina lay beside him, writing furiously in a ring-bound notebook as thoughts fell through the nib of her pen as quickly as they appeared in her head. In the last six months she had started to write down everything, from her own short stories scribbled by flashlight beneath the duvet, to detailing William's dramatic return and the mayhem that followed soon after.

'Oh, yes, I know William personally,' Mrs Cuttle had boasted proudly on the six o'clock news. 'We're actually *very* close friends. I was one of the first people to try his delightful sashimi!'

The country had been obsessed with Merlington, collectively buoyed by the boy with tentacles and his miraculous rescue of the fisherman who had been lost at sea for six years. For a few short weeks, journalists and well-wishers travelled from every corner of the nation, besotted by the barmy seaside town and with all of its fishy inhabitants. They blocked the high street and swamped the seafront, as even the smallest of fishmongers made a fortune thanks to an unusually busy winter season. But then, following a six-way auction for the film rights to William's life story, the bedlam was over just as quickly. The crowded shop-fronts and chaotic streets shrank back to the faces of familiar locals, and the media circus rolled on.

Marina squinted at her notebook with a frown, distracted by the smell of fried haddock beside her as she continued to record memories of William's mouldy old shack. She looked up now, attempting to picture its swaying stilts and peeling wood against the splendour of the town's new pier which was almost finally finished. Poles of sapphire steel extended from the water, supporting a walkway of polished timber that led to a grand pavilion on the pier head. Its glass walls shone in the daylight, like a crystal palace beneath a towering dome of glazed cream tiles. At the entrance, Marina could just about spy the Minnow's Sashimi sign swaying in the breeze.

Sally and Nigel sat beside their daughter on a tartan picnic blanket, an enormous lunchtime spread covering every inch of the fabric. Platters of Minnow's sashimi lay next to a plate of Sole Brothers' scallops, a flask of Clam Baked's famous lobster bisque, and a large pot of mussels from The Codfather. After weeks of struggling to replicate William's sashimi, the town's fishmongers had returned to their speciality offerings with relish as Merlington eased back into the humdrum of everyday life with one wonderful exception – the Minnow family were reunited. For Marina, it felt as though her father had never left, and like William had been part of their lives from the moment that he'd tumbled out of Nigel's old fishing net.

She paused her pen mid-sentence, as a sobering thought frothed at the back of her brain. She listened to the waves, softly lapping at the sand less than a hundred metres from her outstretched feet. The laughter of adults and children alike, as they kicked up the surf or stacked tall sandcastles using bright plastic buckets and long wooden spades ... Merlington had gone back to its own bizarre version of normality without a second's pause. The mystery had been solved, and there were no more clues to be uncovered. Everyone had moved on, as Marina was left to wonder alone whether life would ever feel as magical again.

She slammed the notebook shut and seized her new turquoise flippers, turning to William as he sizzled in the heat before using them to bat away the gulls now nipping at his toes. When he finally woke up and laid eyes on Marina, all eight of his tentacles slightly steaming in the warmth, she snapped a pair of goggles across her face and his groggy expression stretched into an enormous grin.

Nigel leant back on to Sally's shoulder, the two of them beaming while excitement rang across the crowded sand and they watched their children tumble towards the water. Once they stood in the surf, Marina hooked her arms around William's slippery collarbone and he leapt from the shore with a bounce. They sailed over the shallows, faces gawping and fingers pointing in amazement from below, finally landing in the cool depths with a soundless splash. The two friends hurtled together through the sea, rolling and twisting beneath the white-capped waves before shooting from the surface in a somersault of colour, the summer light twinkling on their skin with the brilliance of a thousand iridescent scales.

ACKNOWLEDGEMENTS

My first, massive thank you is to Jazz Bartlett Love – Marina's champion. I am so glad that my entry for the *Times*/Chicken House Fiction Competition landed in your hands, and one day soon I'll get to buy you that drink! I'm hugely grateful to each of the competition judges – Amy Fitzgerald, Nikki Gamble, Gracie Joslin, Becca Langton, Florentyna Martin, Alex O'Connell and Nikesh Shukla – for seeing a spark of potential in my ludicrous story. I am very proud to be the competition's inaugural Chairman's Choice . . . Barry Cunningham, thank you for putting your faith in me. I'll be pinching myself for a long time to come.

Working with Chicken House has been an absolute treat. I could not have asked for a more imaginative, inspiring or talented collaborator than my editor, Kesia Lupo. Thank you for helping me enhance this story, and for all that you have given to Marina and William. Thanks also to Elinor Bagenal, Rachel Hickman, Rachel Leyshon, Laura Myers and each of the Chicken House team for their continued support and enthusiasm. I can't wait to finally visit the coop once the world has reopened.

An enormous thanks to Lauren Gardner, my agent at Bell Lomax Moreton. Your knowledge, patience and generosity in navigating the often daunting, but always exciting publishing process has been so appreciated.

Thank you to Steve Wells for his fantastic design work, and to Maxine Lee-Mackie who brought Marina and William to life with her wonderful cover illustration. You are outrageously talented! I love it more than I would have dared to dream.

The first draft of this novel was quietly written in short fits and starts – on trains, in cafes and at our Bournemouth beach hut – before I finally plucked up the courage to share it with my earliest readers. Lucy Ayrton, Nicky Eaton, Stuart Hurford, Lucy McCormick and Louisa Theobald – thank you for taking the time to sit down with my story, often more than once, when you had no idea if it would be any good. I'm incredibly grateful for your trust, friendship and feedback.

To each of my excellent friends, old and new – thank you for your enduring enthusiasm throughout my journey to publication. Gemma Burnand, Mel

Ezechukwu, Victoria Harris-Wills, Julia Ihnatowicz, Nikesh Patel, Lara Rosenbloom, Piya Sinha-Roy, Rhiannon Sommers, Miranda Want, Adele Zuniga-Villaveces – you have been some of the greatest cheerleaders, along with my London boys and the rest of my Warwick Uni mates. An extra special thank you to Jasbinder Bilan, Holly Rivers, Sam Sedgman and Efua Traoré for their authorly wisdom, and to Isabel Buruma for her expert guidance on sashimi!

I feel very lucky to have such a wonderful family... Thank you Mum and Dad, for supporting me in every way possible. You filled our home with books and movies, let me scream Disney songs in the back seat of the car, and have always made our happiness your number one priority. Thanks also to my big brother Michael, who helped inform my often surreal and sarcastic sense of humour, and to each of my grandparents – Alan, Eric, Norma and Pat – for making our childhood trips to Dorset and Sussex so magical. I will forever be inspired, by the sea in particular, which has always been such an important part of my life.

Finally, the biggest thank you to my brilliant boyfriend, Rob Hayman. For reading my first, unfinished chapters and then every single draft ever since. Without you, I would not have had the courage or confidence to make this dream a reality. Thank you for your boundless support, humour and unending encouragement. You really *are* my favourite.

19/11/21